Searching for Pearly

and Other Secrets

Donna M. Lessard

PublishAmerica
Baltimore

First printing

ISBN: 1-4137-4576-8
PUBLISHED BY PUBLISHAMERICA, LLLP
www.publishamerica.com
Baltimore

Printed in the United States of America

For Amelia
Thanks for all the times you said,
"You need to write that down!"
You've been and remain my greatest inspiration.

Acknowledgments

Many thanks to my sisters, Connie, Cora and Mary, the first to read my little story in its entirety, and to my brother Joe for asking to be next on the reading list. Big thank yous go to Robin Devine and Susanna Brinnon for their excellent advice and editing. I'm also indebted to numerous other members of my community who asked to read my story and offered their feedback. Thanks, Karina. Thank you, Julie and Pete, for your most helpful critiques, and Julie, thank you for the gift of telling the tale to Chloe, the first kid to hear it. Finally, thank you, Devin, for being the first kid to read my story and for being willing to talk to me about it.

Chapter 1

Tamara was just stepping out of her jeans in order to jump into bed when she saw it again—that dim light flickering from the upstairs of the old abandoned Thompson house across the street. From the foot of her bed she advanced the few steps to the window. The screen mesh created a fuzzy view of the tiny light. This marked the fourth time in the past ten days that she had sighted the strange light—strange because no one lived in the Thompson house. No one had for years, according to the realtor who had sold Tamara's house. And strange because there were no cars parked in the driveway or on the street in front of the ancient house.

Tamara made a quick decision and pulled her jeans back on. She stepped quietly into the hallway and glanced at the space under her parents' door. No light—they must be asleep or close to it. She pulled her door closed, grabbed a sweatshirt from an open dresser drawer and surreptitiously raised her window and screen. Just outside was the most beautiful oak tree in the world—well, to a twelve-year-old eye, anyway. One strong branch came right up to Tamara's window. It almost begged her to step out onto its secure, curved surface. Tamara had fantasized about doing just that many times in the last three months, ever since they'd moved into this house. Now she was about to attempt it.

There was no moon out and the September night was warm. The nearest limb was *huge* and had grown as close to the house as it could get without touching. So Tamara was able to swing easily and fearlessly out onto it. A piece of cake! This was truly a wonderful tree for climbing. She was safely on the ground in two minutes.

Looking both ways before crossing the street, less because of possible traffic than because she didn't want to be seen, Tamara ran across the street and squeezed between the thick shrubbery and the left end of the front porch. Just as she reached the cover of the shrubs, she heard voices coming from the near end of the house.

"No, not yet! Wait until we get inside. Someone might see it shining."

"Oh yeah, sorry." Both voices were hushed, not quite whispers, and they sounded like kids.

Tamara assessed her surroundings, trying to determine whether she could sneak around the end of the house without being seen and figure out what those two were doing. She managed to move almost noiselessly to the front corner of the house. Daring a look around it, she saw no one and realized they must have progressed to the backyard. There were no protective bushes at this end of the old place, but Tamara was feeling brave enough with them at the back of the house to creep quietly to the back corner and peek around it. While she couldn't make out their faces, she could see their forms bent over the knob on the back door. One of them seemed to be fiddling with something below the knob, and it didn't appear to be a key—too long for a key. A screwdriver maybe?

"Okay, here goes. Pray it doesn't bounce." Tamara heard a thwack from inside the door as something small hit the floor.

"It landed on the paper!" Kneeling and peering under the door, the kid who had been watching the fiddling spoke excitedly. "Can I pull it out now?"

"Yes, but very slowly, and keep your voice down," the fiddler whispered loudly, quickly scanning the backyard from left to right as though suspecting they might be spied upon. Tamara kept out of sight at the corner of the house and watched as the one boy (definitely a boy's voice) worked with something at the bottom of the door.

"Here it is! It's the key!" Looking up at the fiddler and rising to a standing position at the same time, his voice changed from one of excitement to that of awe. "It worked! I can't believe it! How'd you know that?"

"I told you it would! I'm a genius. Remember?" was the answer, spoken in another definitely boyish voice and a little too loudly for an ongoing act of espionage. More quietly, with a slightly impatient edge, he ordered, "Come on. Let's try it! We don't have a lot of time." Tamara watched as the boy with the key inserted it into the keyhole and turned it.

"Hey, it's turning!" he said just as Tamara heard the click of the lock moving. While trying the knob and opening the door into the old house, he turned toward the other boy. Both boys just stared at each other for a moment.

Taking a deep breath, genius boy said, "Now's the time for those flashlights. Are you ready?"

"Yeah, but I doubt any treasure is just going to be lying around after all these years. How will we know where to look?" There was something familiar in that voice. But what? Nevermind, Tamara needed all of her wits in the moment to continue spying upon the boys without their noticing her.

"Let's just check the place out tonight," genius boy said, glancing at his wristwatch. "Really, my mom's gonna kill me if I'm not home in half an hour. Maybe we'll get some ideas of where to search and what tools we'll need for next time."

Key boy nodded his agreement, though his tone sounded less than enthusiastic. "Yeah, okay." And with flashlights snapped on, they entered the old house, closing the door behind them and shutting inside their flashlight beams.

Man! thought Tamara. *How will I know what they're doing without exposing myself?* She pulled a watch out of her jeans pocket. "Yow!" she said in a loud whisper and quickly recoiled as she remembered her circumstances. But her watch had revealed that it was nearly ten thirty and she needed to be resting for school tomorrow. Still, she didn't want to miss any part of what was going on inside the Thompson house.

She needn't have worried because, within a minute, there was a lot of scuffling coming from inside the house and what sounded like people running. Suddenly the door opened and both boys came almost tumbling out. Key boy barely shut the door behind him in his effort to keep up with genius boy, who was about to leave him in a cloud of dust. They tore right past Tamara, now flattened against the end of the house. In their haste to put distance between them and the house, they didn't even glance in her direction. Tamara took the opportunity presented by their lack of attention to scoot around the corner and use the back of the house for cover in case they did look back. They didn't. They didn't even slow down as far as she could tell. Maybe genius boy wasn't kidding around after all about his mom's penchant for murder over the issue of tardiness.

Now it was really late, and Tamara felt an urgency about getting into her safe warm bed. No one else was wandering the streets of her neighborhood as she warily emerged from the Thompson lot and crossed the street. The sight of her front yard tree excited her, and she couldn't help smiling as she began climbing toward her window. Twelve minutes later, in the warmth and safety of her bed, Tamara was fading into sleep when the difference in appearance between the solid flashlight beams and the dim, flickering light, which she had sighted earlier through the Thompson house upstairs window, tweaked her subconscious.

Chapter 2

In spite of her late night, Tamara awakened refreshed and eager for her day to begin. Even so, the events of the night before kept her preoccupied and quiet throughout breakfast and the bus ride to school.

Since Tamara had moved with her parents to Johnson only three months earlier, at the beginning of the summer, she hadn't made any real friends. In the three weeks she'd been going to Johnson Middle School, she had hung out, sort of, with Mary and Felicia, but really she hardly knew them. The three shared Ms. Bennett's homeroom, and on the first day of school, all three had chosen desks in the middle of the window aisle. So they often chatted mornings before the bell rang, but it was always surface stuff—level of difficulty of tests, whether a teacher seemed fair, amount of homework and such.

This morning Tamara really wasn't listening as Felicia described her weekend exploits babysitting for a neighbor's kids. So she was surprised to look up from her re-examination of the events of the night before to find both girls staring expectantly at her.

"What?"

"Felicia asked you about your weekend, Tamara. You seem a thousand miles away. Are you okay?"

"I'm sorry. I was thinking about something else. But my weekend was spent pretty much reading about Maryland during the Civil War. Not too exciting. Nothing like a four-year-old stuffing a peanut up his nose. I did get to go rollerblading both days, though. That was fun. But

11

it would have been nice to skate with a friend." That last part, though it came from Tamara's mouth, was a complete surprise to her.

"I've got rollerblades," said Felicia. "Why don't you break down and ask a couple of city girls out to your burb next weekend?"

"I've got skates, too," offered Mary, "but I've never tried them. I wanted to take lessons but my parents basically said that wasn't happening until I had a job to pay for the lessons and I should just get real. So how do you two feel about teaching me?"

Felicia and Tamara looked at each other, then twisted their faces into ponderous looks and stared at the ceiling.

"How much is it worth to you?" Felicia was the first to break their silence.

Proving she was sporting enough to go along with their little game, Mary joined them with a ponderous face of her own. "I'll pay your bus fare, round trip." Then, looking at Tamara, she asked, "They do have bus routes out there, don't they?"

"Yes, but hey! What do I get out of this? I don't need bus fare."

It was Felicia and Mary's turn to gang up on Tamara. They looked at each other as though it would be tough coming up with something for Tamara.

"I've got it. You provide lunch for all of us. And make it something worth the trip to the outer limits where you live, girl! I'll bring a surprise to make it all worth your while."

"Hey, all I get is bus fare. I feel ripped off."

"Don't worry," Mary assured Felicia. "You'll get as much from Tamara's surprise as she will. So, is it a deal?" Mary looked from Felicia to Tamara. "Huh?"

"It is by me," said Tamara.

"I'm game," said Felicia.

"All right then. Your house on Saturday?"

"Yeah, at eleven. Okay? I'll have to clear it with my parents, of course."

"Yeah, me too, but eleven sounds good," said Mary.

"I'll ask my dad, but I think he'll be fine with it. He'll probably want to drive out there beforehand," Felicia said, rolling her eyes, "just so he's comfortable knowing where I am. But I think he'll be fine."

"Great. It'll be perfect." Tamara was excited. "My parents have been knocking themselves out trying to locate a lost cemetery. It's a personal pet project of theirs," she added as an aside. "They spend every Saturday researching it. We'll have the house to ourselves."

The bell rang announcing the beginning of homeroom period, and the three girls straightened around in their seats. Tamara didn't run into either of them for the remainder of the day. She felt good about their plan, though, and glad to be making some friends in this new place. Each morning for the rest of the week the three girls talked eagerly about the coming weekend and their skating date. Tamara began looking forward to homeroom period. Her class work for the week was manageable and unexciting, except for Maryland history, which was downright boring. Tamara had to force herself to read the text and practically prop her eyelids open during history class. The text reading took up most of her evenings and it wasn't until Friday night that she found herself perched at the foot of her bed, looking for any sign of light from across the street.

Even so, it took her by surprise when she spied it. The sun had set only moments before and its light was slowly fading on the western horizon. Had she not been looking for it, Tamara probably would not have noticed it, for it was especially difficult to see the dim, flickering light at this time of day. "That's definitely not a flashlight," she found herself saying out loud. Drawing her eyebrows down in a quizzical frown, Tamara watched as the light (a candle?) moved slowly around the room, maybe three feet above the floor. A very short person was looking for something? The treasure mentioned by the flashlight boys on Sunday? Intrigued, Tamara decided to investigate. This time she would go out the front door—no need to attract attention by climbing down the tree this early in the evening.

"I'm taking a walk. Okay?" she asked as she passed through the living room where her parents were watching a video.

"Please take a flashlight. And if you're not back in thirty minutes, I'm coming to find you."

"Make that forty-five minutes please, Mom?"

"Okay, forty-five then. Enjoy."

13

Tamara checked the time on her pocket watch as she let herself out the front door. She knew her mom would be checking the time with the VCR clock, too, and forty-five minutes meant forty-five minutes—not fifty or an hour—to her mom. She wasn't ready to share this mystery with her parents, so she intended to be back before 7:15, no matter what.

The living room blinds were open, so if they looked, her parents could see her crossing the street and going down the driveway of the old Thompson place. While Tamara didn't want to divulge her current plan or last Sunday evening's adventure, she wasn't into spending any energy to actively deceive her parents. If they saw her, they saw her. She would deal with their questions when she got home, *by or before 7:15.* But hopefully they were intent upon their movie, not worrying about their daughter's extra-curricular activities.

Just as she had expected, the back door of the Thompson house was closed but not locked. Key boy had been in too much of a hurry on Sunday to re-lock it. Tamara stepped back into the yard and looked up at the second floor. She could see neither movement nor lights of any kind. Darkness was beginning to descend now. In ten minutes there would be no lingering twilight. Tamara reached into her jacket pocket and touched the tiny flashlight there, as though to reassure herself before walking back to the door. She turned the knob until the door opened. Cautiously she entered the kitchen and stood there for a few moments, listening, while her eyes adjusted to the room's deeper level of darkness. Tamara had decided to leave the flashlight turned off until she really needed it. Slowly she closed the door and looked around.

She could see fairly well. While the appliances seemed dated, everything in the room appeared to be neat and clean. There was no sign of vandalism in this spacious kitchen. She walked slowly through the closer of two interior doorways. The adjacent room she entered was very large, and Tamara's eyes had adjusted enough to the indoor darkness that she could see a huge fireplace on the far wall. There was no furniture in the room. Its floor was covered in carpet, which seemed to be in extremely good condition—its pattern, though, was a very old-fashioned flowery design. On her left a stairway wound upward.

Tamara sucked in her breath and unconsciously held it while she considered the stairs. Had the boys gone up them? Why did they leave so quickly and without locking up? Genius boy seemed to be an attention-to-detail sort of guy. Yet he had *led* their flight from the house and had left the door unlocked. Did something in the house scare them? Would she find a dead body on the stairs?

She let her breath out in a rush. Perhaps it was time for the flashlight. Tamara found her hand had again strayed to the pocket holding it. But instead of turning it on, she walked slowly and quietly toward the stairs. She vaguely noted that the carpet was exceptional in its ability to muffle the sounds of her footsteps. At the bottom of the stairs she stopped and scanned the flight of steps upward. Again, she held her breath, listening for any sounds.

Letting out her breath, Tamara ascended the first two carpet-covered steps. The third step drew her into deeper darkness, and she felt a tightening in her chest as the air became suddenly and inexplicably colder. Possibly a broken upstairs window was causing a draft down the old staircase. All the steps remaining before her were hidden in darkness. But on the left side of the landing above, there was the faintest, flickering glow, barely lighting the landing. Solid walls enclosed the stairwell, concealing the source of the eerie illumination. Slowly Tamara reached into her pocket and pulled out her flashlight. Her heart was racing now. She clicked on the light and the minute click seemed to echo off the stairwell walls. Still no answering sounds were heard. Tamara tore her eyes from the left side of the landing and searched the stairs in front of her for dead bodies. None. Nothing at all on the stairs. And all of the steps appeared to be completely intact—no bottomless pits into which she could fall. She tucked the light back into her pocket to muffle the click before turning it off and proceeded cautiously and with great trepidation up the stairs. In spite of her growing fear, Tamara felt compelled to continue. It was almost as if she couldn't turn back; some unexplainable force drew her to the upstairs of this house.

Semiconsciously counting the steps as she ascended them, Tamara kept her eyes glued to the left side of the landing. The light grew slightly in intensity as she neared the top of the stairs. On the last step, she hesitated. Then, slowly and deliberately, Tamara placed her right foot on the landing, and just as slowly and deliberately, drew up her left foot to join it. Still her gaze was fixed down the left hallway from which the light beckoned. Standing now with both feet firmly on the second floor landing, Tamara could see that the source of the light summoning her came from the second door on the left side of the hallway. That door stood wide open and the light seemed to be dancing just inside the doorway, probably three feet above the floor, just as she had estimated earlier from the safety of her room.

Again Tamara felt brushed by a cold wave of air, and she shivered a little under her light jacket. No way was she walking down the hall to find out what was in that room. "Hello?" she called out tentatively. No answer, no movement, no growls nor threats issued from the room. Again, more self-assuredly, she called out, "Hello?" When an identical lack of response followed, Tamara was reminded of her mom-imposed timeline and looked down to read her watch as she drew it from her pocket. Five before seven registered in her consciousness just as she was swept with another, stronger wave of now almost-freezing air. Startled, she looked up to see—possibly ten feet ahead—a girl not more than six. With her right arm stretched to its length she held in front of her, level with her head, a lighted candle. Its base planted firmly in a candleholder, the candle flame danced eerily, reflecting off the child's drawn scared face.

Chapter 3

Tamara stood frozen in place, unable to do more than stare fixedly, her mouth open. The first words spoken between them came from the little girl. "Please help me," she begged. Tamara continued to stare open-mouthed. Again the little girl begged, "Please help me. I thought you would help me."

"I'm so sorry," Tamara apologized, recovering all at once from her stupor. "I want to help you. My god! Let me take that candle!" Stepping forward, Tamara reached out and gently loosened the candle from the child's small cold hand. "I'm so sorry! I didn't know you were here. I mean I knew or thought someone must be but I didn't for a minute think it could be a little kid. I'm so sorry!" Tamara was wrought with guilt for not knowing something she couldn't possibly have known. "Come here, honey. I'll help you."

The child, whose arm, relieved of the candle, had dropped to her side, turned and walked toward the room with the open door. She spoke agitatedly. "No, I must stay in the closet. It's very important that I stay in the closet. He told me to play quietly in there until he came back. He told me to stay. I promised and I waited for him. He said he'd come back. He said he would."

Tamara had to follow quickly to keep up with her. The little girl went directly to the closet on the far end of the right wall. The closet door stood ajar and she walked right in and sat on the floor.

Tamara was totally confused. She didn't know how to approach the girl with an offering of help that would be acceptable. Kneeling down on the floor of the closet, she set the candle down out of the way and made eye contact with the little girl. "I really want to help you. Please tell me how I can do that."

The girl's face seemed to hold great unhappiness. "I want to find Pearly. Please help me. She was with me in the closet for many days. Now she's gone and I want her back. Will you help me find her?"

Tamara glanced around the closet. Its small size precluded anyone from getting lost in there. "Did Pearly tell you she was leaving? Did she say where she was going? Is Pearly your sister or a friend?"

"Pearly is my doll. She has on a blue dress with real pearl buttons."

Tamara was disconcerted. This wasn't the track she wanted their conversation to take. She pulled out her watch and looked at it—ten after seven. The little girl's eyes had followed Tamara's movements.

"She'll come in five minutes," the girl said quietly. When Tamara looked up at her, the girl's eyes locked with hers in a steady intense gaze. "You know she will and you're the only one I want to talk to. You should go. Please don't tell your mother about me, yet. Use the tree and come back later. Your mother can't help me, Tamara."

Tamara felt another cold rush of air and as the girl's words registered, the hair on Tamara's arms stood up. She stumbled to a standing position.

"How do you know that? How do you know my name?" Tamara demanded.

"Please come back later to help me," the girl repeated, her face drawn with some immense sadness. "I won't go anywhere. Please go. She's getting up now to put on her short, fat, blue coat with no sleeves. Please go *now*." She looked directly into Tamara's eyes as she spoke, and Tamara felt a sense of urgency to do her bidding.

From where she stood, Tamara glanced across the street at her own house. Her mom was getting up from the couch and walking toward the coat closet. Tamara looked back at the child staring up at her. She felt as though she must be in the middle of a bizarre dream, but she turned, anyway, and snapping on her flashlight, she pulled it from her pocket to light her way as she ran out of the room, down the stairs and out of the house. She was just running up her own walkway, when her mother, wearing her new blue down vest, opened their front door. She smiled in surprise at seeing Tamara and said, "Not a moment too soon. How was your walk?"

"All right," Tamara said, walking past her mother, unable to look at either of her parents. "I'm gonna soak in the tub for a while." She headed directly up the stairs, taking them two at a time.

"Okay, dear. There are more Dead Sea salts under the sink. I got some just for you. And we're probably going up to bed in the next half-hour or so. It's going to be another long Saturday for the two of us. I hope that's okay with you."

Halting her bounding up the stairs, Tamara gave her mother a you've-got-to-be-kidding look. "While we're racing around Walker Park we'll try not to grieve at your absence. And later, as we scarf down your lasagna, we'll hold back our tears." Shifting to a tone of sincerity, she said, "Thanks for making it, by the way. I know they'll really like it."

"My pleasure," her mother answered. "We'll leave you a note in the morning."

"I hope you girls have fun," her father offered from his position on the couch, where he waited for her mother to rejoin him. "We'll bring home pizza and you can tell us all about your big day."

"Lasagna *and* pizza on the same day! *Okay, Dad!*" Tamara responded, looking at her mom to see if she would veto his Saturday evening meal plan. But she only suppressed a yawn as she resumed her place on the couch.

"Well, goodnight, you two. Don't stay up too late, now," Tamara teased, resuming her bounding up the stairs. She closed the bathroom door and turned on the water in the tub, throwing in a handful of bath salts from under the sink. She started to slump down on the toilet, caught herself mid-slump and dropped the toilet lid before letting her butt fall onto it.

With her left elbow resting on her left knee and her chin resting on her fist, Tamara stared at the rushing water filling the bathtub. What was happening with her? Taking orders from a little kid? No doubt a missing kid! I've left her, she thought, all by herself in an abandoned old house. Mom and Dad would go through the roof if they knew. That's another thing—why haven't I told them? There's a little, lost kid hanging out in the old place across the street, and I've let them watch their video like nothing's going on.

She got up to test the water temperature and adjusted the flow before stripping and getting tentatively into the tub. When she felt comfortable with the temperature, she sat down, then let herself slide under the water until her head was immersed. She burst headfirst back up through the water's surface and rested against the back of the tub. She breathed in deeply, savoring the scent of eucalyptus, then sighed.

There was no escaping the truth. The girl knew Tamara's name before Tamara told her and she knew what her mother was going to do before she did it. If she had seen Tamara from the upstairs window, she could have known where Tamara lived and that Tamara had recently climbed out her window to the tree. But how could she know her name or when her mother was rising from the couch? There must be some explanation that made sense. But nothing Tamara could come up with explained the girl's knowledge of those things.

And who dressed the poor kid? Her dress, though clean and untorn, was so outdated, it would have been rejected for resale by Goodwill and the Salvation Army. Who lets their kids run around without shoes in the world today? Was she homeless? Would that explain her outfit and lack of shoes?

Tamara heard her parents coming up the stairs. Even more difficult than understanding the child's behavior was coming up with an explanation of her own behavior this evening—and the behavior she was about to display once she felt reasonably sure her parents were in bed for the night. Well, she would just get to the bottom of this, find out the child's circumstances and explain it to her parents. Once the situation was understood and dealt with, surely they would get over the fact that Tamara knew the little girl had taken up residence in an abandoned house hours before she reported it to them. *Not!* She would just have to face that later. She couldn't think about it now. It was taxing just trying to figure out the girl and what to do to help her.

After soaking and worrying for over half an hour, Tamara got out of the tub and into her terrycloth robe. As she walked down the hall to her room, she saw that the lights were on in her parents' room. It was still early for a Friday. They would probably be up for another hour or more. Once inside her own room, she closed the door and crossed to the window. There it was, flickering, but definitely there, calling her to get more deeply involved. It was going to be difficult to stay focused on something else for an hour. Reading *anything* was out of the question. Tamara looked around her room. Doing something physical might keep her from leaping out the window with impatience. The girls were coming tomorrow. It wouldn't hurt to clean up her room, an activity for which the opportunity was never quite right—until this moment. She began attacking a pile of clothes that had been growing in front of her closet until the door could not be opened.

Just over an hour later, as Tamara was organizing her desk to perfection, her mom stopped in to say goodnight.

"Damn!" her mom swore good-naturedly. "Your friends won't believe you're really a seventh-grade human child when they see this!"

"Hey, here's that Lauren Hill CD you wanted to listen to—in July, wasn't it?"

Laughing—at Tamara's expense—they kissed goodnight. After her mother left, Tamara kept working on her desk until it was finished, then spent a few minutes straightening her dresser top. A quick check of the hall revealed that the bathroom night light was the only thing illuminating it. Tamara hurriedly dressed in a pair of jeans and a sweater she found hanging over the back of her desk chair. Then she pulled on a pair of sneakers. Opening the window, she realized she had left the flashlight in the bathroom. She hesitated. Man! She really didn't want to go back down the hall, and the three flashlights she had uncovered in the last hour and a half all needed new batteries. Oh well, there was enough of a moon tonight to enable her to see while climbing down the tree. It just might be a little scary at the Thompson house without a light. But she could do it; she *was not* going back to the bathroom to get the one in her jacket pocket. She pushed up the screen and climbed out into the tree. Three minutes later she was inside the old house again. She wanted to call out to the girl but realized she had never asked her name.

Tamara breathed in and out slowly and consciously three times. Then she moved toward the faintly visible doorway leading to the large living room. She stopped when she got to the doorframe and faced toward the dark staircase. Again Tamara drew in a deep breath, held it and walked quickly toward the stairs. She began breathing again as she started up the steps. As before, the left side of the landing above was faintly lit. Growing a little more confident of herself and what lay before her, Tamara quickened her pace to the landing. At the top, she again grew wary and called out, "It's me, Tamara. Are you there, little girl?" The light that had been coming from the second room on the left now spilled across the hallway, followed by the girl, holding her candle.

"Thank you for coming back," was all she said before she turned back into the room. Wanting to be where there was light, Tamara hurried after her. Looking around the dimly lit room, she noted that everything seemed just as she had left it earlier. The child was looking intently at her.

"I don't know your name," said Tamara. "Somehow you know mine, but I don't know yours. So what *is* your name?"

"Sarah."

"Ah, Sarah, a very pretty name. What's your last name, Sarah?"

Hesitating, as though she had to think about the answer, "Thompson," she responded.

"What a coincidence! This is the old Thompson house! You've chosen to hide in a house owned by people with the same last name!"

Sarah cocked her head and looked askance at Tamara. Her face no longer seemed laden with sadness. Perhaps she was starting to trust that Tamara would get her safely home.

"I should have brought you something to eat. You must be hungry."

"Please help me find Pearly."

"Sarah," Tamara started over, getting down on one knee so that her face was level with Sarah's. "I'll look for Pearly, but I need to know how you got inside this house when it was locked up, and who you were referring to when you said 'he' told you to stay in the closet. And where is he now? Were you talking about your father?"

"Father told me to wait in the closet."

"Where is he now, Sarah?"

"Mama said Ruben Corey shot him."

"Who is Ruben Corey?" Tamara was worrying again that she was mishandling the situation by not calling in higher authorities. "Where's your mother? Where is your father now? In the hospital?"

"In the cemetery. Mama said Thomas buried him there by Rebecca. That was before Thomas found me in the closet. Then he sent us away so Ruben Corey or the others wouldn't hurt us. I didn't have time to go back for Pearly."

Tamara felt like she was wallowing in a quagmire of unsolicited information that neither went together nor helped her to figure out how to help Sarah.

"How long ago was your father shot, Sarah?"

"It was in May 1863." Sarah was again looking directly into Tamara's eyes.

Tamara put her other knee on the floor and sat back on her heels as she considered Sarah's face and her answer. Sighing, she looked up briefly into the room's nearest dark corner. Then, resigned to the strangeness of the situation but determined to understand it, she looked back at Sarah. Her head was swimming with bits and pieces of information.

"I want to help you. I do. Please sit down here and tell me everything from when your dad told you to stay in the closet. I want to know why he told you to stay in this closet in this house." Tamara paused briefly, then asked, "Sarah, is this your house?"

"No."

"Then whose house is it?"

"This is my father's house."

Surprised and confused, Tamara pointed out, "But you just said it wasn't your house."

"It's not. It belongs to Father—and Thomas."

"What about your mother?"

"My mother's name was Annie Free Thompson."

Tamara looked at Sarah for a long time, trying to realign pieces of information so that they fit together in some kind of sensible way. "Didn't the house belong to your mother as well as your father?"

"No."

Thinking suddenly that she might have found two pieces that fit together, Tamara asked, "Sarah, was she a slave? Your mother, was she a slave?"

"Yes—once—before I was born."

"Who is the other person you mentioned as part owner of this house?"

"Thomas. Thomas, my brother."

"Your brother was part owner but not your mother? I thought I was beginning to understand but I don't. I *so* don't."

"I think you do understand, Tamara, but you don't want to believe."

A cold draft of air swept through the room and Tamara shivered. Sometimes Sarah seemed a child of six; sometimes she spoke as one far older. Tamara hugged herself for warmth and searched Sarah's face for a clue to make everything that Sarah spoke understandable in a way that was everyday, usual, down to earth, normal. She longed for an answer to lead her away from the bizarre conclusions coming together in her mind. Sense? No, it didn't make any sense of a usual sort. If she spoke aloud the thoughts she was resisting, her sanity might be in doubt.

Tamara readjusted herself until she was sitting fully on the floor with her legs crossed in front of her. Resting her elbows on her knees, she looked away from Sarah and rubbed both hands down over her eyes and face until her fingers met over the bridge of her nose. With fingers interlocked as though in prayer, she sat back straightening her spine and letting her hands fall into her lap. She sighed and looked at Sarah again.

"Your mother, who was once a slave, and Mr. Thompson, who owned this house, gave birth to you in eighteen fifty something. One day your father left you alone inside the closet with strict instructions to stay there until he came back. Only he never *came* back. You had your doll, Pearly, with you. As soon as your brother Thomas found you hiding in the closet, he sent you and your mother away somewhere safe from the people who killed your father and might try to hurt you. In the rush, Pearly got left behind and she's so important...."

Tamara paused and looked Sarah over from head to toe as though she was scanning her for reproduction someplace else. She sighed again. Then, with a slow resignation, she continued, "She's so important, you've come back from the dead to find her."

For the first time that night Sarah smiled—a shy, enigmatic smile. And Tamara felt chilled to the bone by another sudden and unexplainable cold draft of air sweeping through the room.

Chapter 4

Tamara was adding the final touches to a salad fit for royalty—three royals, to be exact—and keeping an eye out for Felicia and Mary when she spotted them walking leisurely down the sidewalk. Both wore full backpacks, and Mary carefully carried in her outstretched arms something housed in a brown paper grocery bag lying on its side. She saw them looking for the house number and ran out to greet them.

"Sorry about the missing numbers. Mom and Dad keep promising to replace them and never seem to find the time. I'll probably get to it before they do. I guess you didn't have any trouble with the bus routes. You're right on time. I just finished making a great salad." Tamara had become a regular Chatty Cathy at the sight of her two new friends. Until that moment she hadn't been aware of how much she was looking forward to spending the afternoon with them.

"Got room in your freezer for the after-lunch surprise?" Mary asked. "If necessary, I can take it out of this paper bag, but *no one* gets to peek before lunch."

"Great, 'cause I didn't make any dessert. I thought you might be bringing one. I hoped you were. Does it absolutely have to go in the freezer?"

"Actually, the refrigerator will be fine."

Both girls followed Tamara into her kitchen where she immediately checked the freezer. "Do you think there's room?" Tamara asked, opening the door as wide as it would go so that Mary could assess the available space.

"Oh yeah, I think so. I'll take it out of the bag." Doing so, Mary looked around for a place to deposit the bag and settled for the table, when she realized Tamara and Felicia were totally involved in ogling the surprise.

"Ooh, definitely pie-shaped," said Felicia, grinning at Tamara.

"Okay, I'm not answering any questions about my surprise," Mary warned as she stuffed her pie-shaped object, swaddled in aluminum foil, into the open freezer. She closed the door quickly and changed the subject. "Where are we skating? On the sidewalks around here? I really haven't done this before. You two can't let me get run over. All right?"

"Trust us," Felicia said, grinning impishly and slanting her eyes toward Tamara.

Tamara picked up on Felicia's cue. She draped an arm over Mary's shoulders to draw her out the kitchen door and with fake warmth said, "Oh yes, dear. You're in good hands with the skating instructors of Johnson Middle School."

"Is that anything like the skating instructors from Hell?" Mary asked as she was forced out the door, dragged by Tamara and pushed from behind by Felicia.

Two hours later the three girls, tired but excited and very hungry, tumbled back through Tamara's kitchen door. They eagerly shed themselves of their skating gear, leaving it in a pile in a corner of the living room, and washed up in anticipation of the promised luncheon feast and the titillating surprise. Clean and hungry, Tamara and Felicia entered the kitchen where Mary had just released the dessert from the freezer. It was now at rest on the island countertop. Drops of condensation covered the aluminum foil, only further whetting Tamara and Felicia's appetites and imaginations. Tamara heated individual portions of her mother's famous spinach lasagna in the microwave and put out the salad and bowls, while Mary and Felicia set the table. When Tamara announced that all was ready, they plunked themselves down at the table and dug in. After savoring the first few mouthfuls, they began recounting their skating foray through the park. Eventually their talk turned to school things.

"Hank Hanley is my choice so far," said Mary.

"My dad wants to know why there aren't any girls running for class president. I think he'd like me to run but that's not my thing," offered Felicia, wrinkling her nose.

"Something about Hanley bothers me," said Tamara. "I'm impressed that he has enough on the ball to have everything he says translated into Spanish. That's a nice touch and no one else has even bothered to follow his lead on that. But I don't know. It also kind of bothers me that he doesn't do his own translating."

"He's in my Spanish class, and believe me, you wouldn't want to hear him speak Spanish. He comes close to ruining the language for me, and you know how much I love Spanish. His interpreter is very good, by the way," Mary volunteered.

"Anyway, Tamara, what are you talking about?" asked Felicia. "It's not like you know one word of Spanish other than 'taco' and 'tamale.' Why are you criticizing him for that?"

"Okay, okay, point taken. You're right. I don't speak Spanish. Okay, well, he's too smooth or something."

"He's a baby politician," Mary said. "And I think he intends to grow up to be a big one—as in White House big. But really he's the only one running who has anything real to say. And I'm impressed by the Spanish thing, Tamara. I am."

"I'm with Mary on that. Maybe he does need to tone down his image, though. That smooth thing comes across as weaselly from time to time."

"Yeah, I guess it's that," said Tamara. "Maybe he really is White House material."

"Hey, speaking of the White House, did you know that some parts of it might be haunted?" Mary asked. "I read an article about it in an old magazine while I waited for my dentist last week. It was at least five years old. I'm not kidding! Why do they keep magazines that old in waiting rooms?"

"You mean by ghosts?" Felicia asked, ignoring Mary's last question.

"Yes, by ghosts. The Clintons never reported any sightings, but other White House staff members, throughout the years, have. Many people have seen Lincoln's ghost. And President Truman answered a knock at his door one night but no one was there. So he *said*. But he told people it had been President Lincoln. Now why did he say that?"

"Maybe he got the idea from other people's ghost stories. Maybe he was kidding around and he got quoted out of context," said Felicia. "What do you think, Tamara? Do you believe in ghosts?"

"Me? I—I do. I do actually believe in spirits or ghosts haunting places. I'm not sure what it means when they do, but I definitely believe they appear to people."

"No need to get all serious about it, Tamara," teased Felicia. "What makes you such a believer?"

Tamara's response to Felicia was to not respond but to question Mary further. "What else did the article say? Did it go deeper than just reporting people's so-called sightings? Anything about why, for instance, Lincoln would roam the White House knocking on doors?"

"Naturally, once I found an interesting article, the hygienist called me in. As far as I read, though, it said he'd appear whenever the U.S. might be in trouble, security-wise. Man! I wonder if he wandered the halls before nine-eleven and they're keeping it a big secret!"

"Now that's a possibility. If a current president sees an old, *dead* president walking around, you bet the Secret Service will keep that quiet," said Felicia, "at least until they retire and write a book about that and all the other weird things that go on in the White House." Looking from Tamara to Mary and back at Tamara, Felicia said, "Earth to Tamara—have we lost you? Is there something deep going on inside your brain or are you thinking, like me, that it's show time for the surprise? I'm totally ready for dessert. What about you two?"

Tamara surfaced from her pondering, smiled affectionately at Felicia and turned to Mary. "I'm ready for the unveiling, too. What do you say?"

Mary smiled with self-pride at her friends. "Do let me serve you, my dears." Pushing herself away from the table, she walked to the island in the middle of the kitchen and, with her back turned to her curious and eager friends, she uncovered her creation. Turning with it in her hands and walking toward them, she announced, "Made with love for my two most excellent friends—and me, of course—fresh, home-made peanut butter pie!"

Tamara and Felicia's eyes widened at the sight. An entire pie—and no mere pie, but a luscious-looking, coffee-colored, creamy confection covered with peanuts and flakes of dark chocolate—was placed before them. Their oohs and ahs and other exclamations of delight broadened the proud smile on Mary's face where she stood over them with her hands clasped behind her back, basking in the array of adulation. Eyes still glued to the pie, Felicia was barely able to choke out, "Where's the knife, Tamara?"

Mary's pie, tasting as luscious as it looked, put an end to their skating for the afternoon. After lounging lazily in front of a video for two hours and playing a game of Scrabble, the three girls strolled to the bus stop, four blocks from Tamara's house. Their day together had cemented their budding friendship, and they were not ready to say good-bye until forced to do so by the arrival of the bus. Finding empty curbside seats, Mary and Felicia turned in unison to wave through the window to Tamara. Returning their waves, Tamara watched until the bus pulled out into traffic, then turned for her solitary walk home. Her parents would be home soon. Needing to prolong and share the perfection of her day, she looked forward to seeing them. Walking toward the western horizon, which had been rose pink on the walk to the bus stop and was now blazing red, Tamara sorted through the activities of the day, savoring each part, reliving the highlights and perfecting the telling of a normal Saturday in the normal life of a normal twelve-year-old girl.

Chapter 5

Sunday morning. Ah, Sunday morning—the beginning of Tamara's favorite day of the week, if her homework is completed and no household duties are hanging over her. Such was the case this Sunday morning. She was free to do whatever activity she chose. There had been Sundays in winter when Tamara had never changed out of her pajamas, had barely risen to prowl the kitchen and scavenge food to bring back to her room where she munched and read the day away. This Sunday morning Tamara had awakened with the first rays of the sun. Now she turned over, grabbed her extra pillow and hugged it to her, sighing and sinking into its cool softness. This Sunday would not be a day spent reading in bed. No, today would be another day of activity like yesterday. Only, unlike yesterday, today's activities would have more to do with the paranormal than the normal world.

She closed her eyes and recalled Friday evening's visit with Sarah. The girl had related a remarkable tale of fear, love, loss and hatred, occurring one hundred forty years before. She told her story as seen through the eyes of a six-year-old child caught in a world of confused boundaries among Blacks and Whites, friends, neighbors, enemies, relatives, gray soldiers and blue soldiers, emancipators and enslavers. Clearly, trust was not a thing easily established in the world outside of her childhood home. She recounted a vivid tale of a child loved and protected by a family of unusual make-up and governance for the times. Her mother, a former slave, had lived as Benjamin Thompson's wife on his isolated farm. Thomas, Thompson's older child by his deceased wife, seemed an integral and loved member, as well, of this unusual family. Sarah's every reference to him was spoken with great affection. Her father and older brother had obviously doted on her in every way possible. But in 1863, threatened by the hatred generated by a long-standing feud and the dangers posed by the turmoil of civil war, the Thompson men felt impelled to get Sarah and her mother away to the safety of Canada, at least until the end of the war was declared. Sarah's mother was packing a wagon with supplies for their journey, when Benjamin apparently found it imperative to leave the house. For some unexplained reason, he chose to leave his six-year-old, playing hide from Mommy, while he completed his errand. He left her with strict instructions to play quietly in his closet and to answer to no one until he returned. Since he was murdered that morning, he never returned to release Sarah from her closet hideout. According to Sarah, it was three days before Thomas found her hiding in the closet. Tamara didn't understand how that could happen. Her own parents would have been frantically opening and closing every door in the house over and over again, had six-year-old Tamara been lost in the house. "But the closet is a secret that only Father and I knew," she had said when Tamara questioned her. "They didn't know where to look and the latch is up too high for me. I can't reach it."

"Couldn't you hear Thomas and your mother calling for you?"

"It's so quiet in there. Father made it that way. And I promised to stay until he came back," she had said, her voice grown distant.

Tamara had given up questioning her on the subject but remained unclear as to why the door wasn't ripped open and Sarah found upon news of her father's death. She couldn't picture them walking past the door without checking it. Three days was a long time to go with only water and apples for nourishment. Once Sarah was discovered, her mother ministered to her needs and prepared her for their trip north. From Sarah's description of the event, everyone was in rush mode and Sarah remained somewhat dazed from her extended ordeal alone in the closet. By the time she remembered Pearly, they were too far along on their journey to turn back. On Friday evening, the ghostly Sarah had begged Tamara to search the house for the lost doll, and Tamara had agreed. She would search every nook and cranny during the day Sunday. Of course, it made sense that the doll had been thrown or given away about one hundred thirty-nine years before, but Tamara did not risk further agitating Sarah with that speculation.

The smell of freshly brewed coffee made Tamara keenly aware of her empty stomach. She dressed and joined her parents in the kitchen. After breakfast with them, Tamara slipped out to begin her search at the Thompson house. Slipping away was an easy task, since her parents were still very excited about their neighborhood cemetery project. They had left the Sunday paper strewn over the living room and the remains of breakfast on the table in order to get to their computers for some early morning Internet research. Amused by their unusual intensity for this mutual project, Tamara cleaned up the kitchen before leaving the house, even though it wasn't one of her weekend responsibilities.

And so once again she found herself inside the kitchen door of the Thompson house. It felt strange to be there so early in the day, with sunlight streaming in through the uncurtained kitchen windows. Though not as brightly illuminated as the kitchen, the living room and all its details were easy to see and examine at this hour. The house felt friendlier, less scary at this time of day.

Tamara stood in the kitchen-to-living room doorway and looked around the large room. If not for the carpet, the room might feel daunting, but the carpet seemed to soften it, make it more welcoming. She wasn't very hopeful that she would find the doll there or anywhere, for that matter. After all, it wasn't as though there were piles of clutter to dig through. As much as she'd seen so far, the house was clutter free—no furniture behind which to lose any playthings. But it was time to move, to start fulfilling her promise to the little spirit child. Tamara wanted very much to give Sarah her longed-for doll. She couldn't let her fear of failure prevent her from even beginning the search. So she moved forward toward the huge fireplace she had noticed upon her first foray into the house.

It was a truly massive structure, extending from floor to ceiling and making up a third of the wall. Most eight-year-olds could walk into it and stand under the chimney without bumping their heads on the stonework. It was huge! And in great condition. Tamara reached out and touched the smooth, cool surface of the stones. She stood back and studied the entire fireplace, imagining the mantle with photographs and knick-knacks belonging to Sarah's family spaced atop it. She wondered whether her childhood in this house had been happy or one fraught with fear and worry.

She forced her thoughts back to the present and the task at hand. Scanning the empty room, she eyed the window seats on either side of the fireplace. Tamara's eyes widened. Window seats seemed such an old-fashioned, Jane Austen piece of architecture. She walked to the seat on the left side of the fireplace and sat down tentatively. Smiling to herself, she pushed back into the corner of the window. Drawing her feet up onto the sill, she hugged her knees, and sighing, rested her chin upon them. She closed her eyes and tried to picture the room with furniture, pictured herself as a curious six-year-old on a Sunday morning. The heavy drapes, warmed by the sunlight they so efficiently blocked, felt comforting against Tamara's skin where they touched her hand and face. She sighed again at the sensual pleasantness of the moment.

Opening her eyes, she let them wander slowly around the room. No clues jumped out at her. It was a large, empty room with occasional yellowed squares, where pictures must have once hung against the old wallpaper. No hiding places here. Time to move on to another room. As Tamara reluctantly stood to leave the room, she looked down to admire the window seat. How cool it would be to have one in her own house. Imagining that, she remembered that window seats often served the functional purpose of storage. Using both hands, palms up, she gently lifted against the leading edge of the seat. It didn't budge and Tamara slumped in disappointment. She knew she was letting herself be sidetracked by the intrigue the old seats held for her. It was easy to be sidetracked considering how futile her mission for Sarah seemed. Maybe the lid was just heavy. She tried again to lift it, putting more muscle into the effort. But the window seat did not give at all.

Not being one to do a job halfway, Tamara could not leave the room until she had tested the top of the other window seat. Exerting some muscle once again she tried lifting the seat on the right of the fireplace. To her surprise, it gave, and Tamara's heartbeat increased slightly as she opened the lid to a forty-five degree angle. She found herself staring down into a rectangular, cedar-lined box, probably eight feet long. It still retained the slight scent of cedar, appealing to her olfactory senses. But the box was disappointingly empty. She closed the lid and looked over at the other seat. Why would one box serve the secondary purpose of storage space and the other act only as a seat hiding useless space? That didn't make sense. People used everything available in the old days. She opened the lid again and let it rest against the drapes while she carefully inspected the rim of the box. The catch to secure the lid was located on the box portion of the seat and had been worn into a groove. Tamara could see that the latch no longer worked as it had been intended to work and realized that was the only reason she had been able to open this window seat. She pulled the lid forward and examined the inside edge of the lid.

Tamara stood in that position, absently staring at the groove on the box while she worked and reworked the latch mechanism on the lid. Slowly she turned her gaze up to watch the latch mechanism as her right hand operated it over and over. This wasn't making sense either. The lever operating the latch was located *inside* the lid. Had the catch not been broken, the only way to open the lid was from *inside* the box.

Tamara became suddenly alert and scrutinized the inside lip of the lid. The latch was attached to a metal band fitted against the right inside lip. The band was equipped with more metal parts at the corner but continued around the corner of the lid, ending where the short side of the lid ended—at the wall hinge. Feeling along the band from the latch to the hinge, Tamara wondered at its purpose. The latch operated perfectly from the left side of the latch mechanism. Why would anyone add extraneous pieces to the opposite side?

To open it from the outside! Of course!

The end of the metal band was molded to a two-inch, solid, rectangular, metal cube protruding through the lip to the outside edge.

Moving closer to the right end of the box, Tamara pushed on the metal cube and watched the latch mechanism move to its release position. She depressed the cube over and over, watching the latch move from release to catch position. Abandoning that seat, she directed her attention to the other one.

"Yes!" she whispered as she moved to the left end of the other window seat. Sure enough there was a metal cube, seemingly a decorative effect, embedded in the seat lip. Tamara pushed on the cube with her left thumb and pulled up against the seat edge with her right hand. The lid gave, responding heavily, but opening as she continued lifting. Again there was the faintest aroma of cedar. Folded neatly in the fireplace end of this box was an old quilt. It seemed to be in good shape but was definitely old, hand stitched. Tamara reached in with both hands to lift it out of the box in order to examine it. As she did so, the knuckles of her right hand brushed against the panel constituting the end of the box. The panel moved slightly and Tamara thought she must have broken it loose. She removed the quilt to the floor in front of the window seat and bent into the box to see if she'd damaged its right end. Pressing her fingertips against the lower edge to test its strength, she felt the panel give outward as though it was attached at the bottom by some sort of spring-loaded hinge, allowing the panel's top to open in and down. She was suddenly looking into a dark space where the end panel of the box should have come into contact with the fireplace stonework. Tamara bent down and peered into the space. It was about a foot deep and as tall as the box. It contained three articles—a small, strange-looking lantern, an old, dry, stiffened leather pouch and a rolled piece of fabric, tied with yarn. Tamara closed and re-opened the end panel. Then she closed it again and studied the appearance of the box. Had she not accidentally pushed against the bottom of the panel, she would never have discovered the opening beyond it. It wasn't meant to be discovered; it was a secret space, a hiding place. Why? Tamara opened the secret panel again. She wanted to study the items in the hiding place more closely but didn't feel that to be an acceptable action. Her parents, both archeologists, had drummed into her head that unprofessional handling of antique artifacts could damage or destroy them forever. And Tamara believed she was looking at something very old and valuable—at least to a museum curator or historian.

She closed the panel and turned to the quilt lying on the floor. She probably shouldn't have touched it either but hadn't considered its possible age at the time she lifted it out of the box. Without unfolding it, she looked closely at its repeated pattern. The background of each quilt square was light blue and contained an inch-thick, dark-blue outline of a smaller square. To Tamara, thinking geometrically, it looked like each corner of the dark-blue outline was overlaid with a dark-blue triangle, the apex of which coincided with the inside corner of the smaller square. She found it strange and wondered how anyone thought up quilt patterns. Gently, she placed the quilt back where she had found it.

She returned to the window seat on the right of the fireplace. Propping the lid against the window, she tested the panel end near the fireplace. It opened like the other to expose an identical, secret compartment, housing a lantern, a leather pouch and a rolled and tied piece of fabric. She closed the compartment and the lid and sat upon it. The whole thing was becoming more complicated. She had hoped to look for Sarah's doll and be finished. But someone needed to know about the items in the secret compartments. Well, she'd just have to figure that out later. As exciting as this interlude had been, she had to resume her search for Pearly. She still had the rest of the house to go through, regardless of how futile it felt.

And go through it she did, but without any more discoveries. The most interesting thing was that the closet in the master bedroom was, by far, the smallest of all the bedroom closets. Perhaps Benjamin Thompson was an unprepossessing sort of rich guy. She supposed he *must* have been rich. His house was very large and very well built. She wondered whether he had had one of those large, old-fashioned, freestanding closets, whatever they were called, to hold the majority of his clothes. Whatever the reason, the house was built with more generous closet space in every room but his.

It was after noon and Tamara was hungry when she finished with the kitchen, the last room in her search. She hadn't encountered Sarah anywhere. Indeed, she had been relieved as she opened the closet door in the master bedroom to inspect it and had not found Sarah's forlorn, little face staring up at her. The bedroom and closet hadn't looked much different than they had on Friday night, aside from being lighted by the midday sun. A small circle of light, cast on the left wall of the master bedroom, had betrayed a knothole in the closet wall. She supposed sunlight must have been shining through from the adjacent bedroom's windows. That circle, of course, had not been visible at night.

Tamara took one last look around the kitchen as she reached for the doorknob. She was surprised, in an unconscious sort of way, to feel it turn in her hand before she had had a chance to apply any pressure. Before she knew what was happening, the door hit her hard in the forehead. Stunned by pain, clutching her head in both hands, she stumbled backwards, crying out, "Aaahh, god! Oh, my god!"

Through the cloud of pain in her head, Tamara heard the pounding of running feet hitting the lawn. When she was able to get herself out the door, she barely caught a glimpse of flying feet and flapping jackets as two ball-capped kids ran around the corner and down the street—in the same direction two boys had run on Sunday evening one week ago.

Chapter 6

Felicia and Mary stared open-mouthed at Tamara on Monday morning. Tamara had tried her best, resorting to a baseball cap, to hide the bruise in the middle of her forehead, but the disguise didn't fool her friends.

"What in the hell happened to you?" Felicia voiced the feelings of both of them.

"Did you do that skating?" Mary wanted to know.

Tamara had tried to think up elaborate excuses to tell them, but in the end, she decided that the truth was probably best. She thought she could do it without telling them about Sarah. There was no way she could keep up with a lie and what if they asked her questions she hadn't covered in a made-up scenario? If it seemed like she was lying, some well-intentioned teacher might get the notion her parents had mistreated her. She didn't need that kind of aggravation and her parents certainly didn't.

"It's a long story, but in the end I get hit in the head by a rudely opened door."

"Not enough details, Tamara. We want everything." Felicia was leaving no room for misunderstanding. So Tamara told them the whole story leaving out Sarah, which was a lot, and let them think she had been searching for the "treasure" mentioned by the boys on the first night. They got very interested and were asking for more details when the principal's voice over the intercom silenced the buzz in the room.

"More later," Tamara promised, turning in her chair.

"As you all know, you will have an opportunity during lunch and after last period to vote for class officers. Right now each candidate will have two minutes to make a last appeal to each of you. We'll start the slate with Michael Harrington for president of the seventh grade."

Tamara listened to each candidate for office. She wasn't sure how seriously to treat school government in the seventh grade but she intended to vote and wanted to have as much information as possible. Remembering their Saturday conversation about his possible sleazy streak, she listened to Hank Hanley with her eyes turned toward the ceiling. But when his interpreter began, "Mis amigos" was all that Tamara heard. Something had clicked into place; a neuron had synapsed at just the right moment.

"Oh my god," she breathed, spreading her hands and turning to Mary behind her. "It's him, his voice. He's the one! From that first night at the house! Remember? I thought there was something familiar about him? He's Hank's translator! Who is he, anyway?"

"Tamara, have the courtesy to be quiet until the speakers are all finished, please." Ms. Bennett looked at her with surprise and annoyance at the same time.

Tamara, shocked by her own behavior, turned to face forward and tried to make herself smaller at her desk as she mouthed, "Sorry." She felt Mary's pat of support on her shoulder as she slunk down in her seat.

There was barely enough time for all the candidates from both grades to have their say before the bell rang for first period class. So the three girls were unable to confer over Tamara's newest information.

"Lunch—first or second today?" she asked them both as the homeroom class filed out the door and spilled into the halls.

"Second," answered Mary, "but I'm voting during lunch. You will be, too, Tamara. Right?" That sounded more like a directive than a question affording alternative actions.

"Oh yeah, I'm first lunch but I'll be voting. Sorry," said Felicia.

"Me, too. How could I forget already?" Tamara really wanted to get together with them and discuss this new turn now that she had practically leveled with them about her weekend activities.

"Tomorrow morning then. Don't do anything without telling us, Tamara!" Felicia was adamant. "Have you considered that it might not be safe? Your purple, bulging forehead a case in point. What did you tell your parents about that? Do you really have parents, Tamara?" Turning aside to Mary and moving up next to her so that their shoulders touched conspiratorially, she said, "Think about it, Mary. Have we ever seen her alleged parents or even pictures of them?"

Laughing in spite of herself, Tamara pulled down on her cap visor. "They think I've developed an attachment to hats and taken a sudden interest in that history paper I've been putting off for a week. I spent most of the rest of the day in my room. One good thing is that I actually *did* start on my paper. I had to do *something* to pass the time. Okay, then—first thing in the morning, Felicia. And don't be dragging in, either!" As Felicia separated from them at the end of the corridor, Tamara asked Mary, "Just how weird *do* I look?"

"For starters, couldn't you have found a cap that said something usual like the Baltimore Orioles instead of 'Save the manatees'?" Mary asked, grinning wickedly, just before ducking into her first period class. Tamara was destined to spend the day self-consciously aware of her appearance.

❧

"What did your parents say last night?" were the first words out of Felicia's mouth the next morning.

"I was able to tell them what happened while leaving out a few minor details they forgot to ask—like where, when, why." Tamara recalled her parents' stunned looks when they got home from work and saw their daughter sporting a large, swollen, multi-colored contusion in the middle of her forehead. She explained right away that she'd been hit accidentally with a door opening in, just as she was attempting to exit.

"Well, who did it? Did they stop to see if you were okay? Or even just apologize?" Her mother was aghast.

"No. He ran in the other direction, but I think I know who it was."

"You could have gone to the nurse. And I'm surprised that a teacher didn't send you. Was there a teacher present when it happened?"

"No, not for miles. And, Mom, I have no one to blame but myself. I didn't even think about showing it to the nurse." (All true. Everything she told them was absolutely true.) "Once I saw how bad it looked, I just wanted to hide it. It's starting to hurt now. How do you suggest I treat it? Ice? Arnica?" (Get them off the subject by any means possible.)

"Both. It should have been done already. Oh, Tamara, that's gotta hurt a lot!"

"It hurts *me* just looking at it," her father interjected, rubbing a hand across his forehead. "Damn, Tamara! Do I need to go straighten out some rude boy?"

"Dad, no! Don't even kid about that!"

"Then I'll go get the arnica while Mom's fixing the ice," he said, departing in the general direction of their bathroom medicine cabinet.

They applied the arnica and ice and babied her while she did her homework. They told her all about their research on the local private cemetery, which turned out to be the Thompsons' plot. Vaguely interested, Tamara listened, asked a few questions and, mostly, was glad they had stopped asking *her* questions about the incidentals of her head injury. Plus, being pampered for an evening was nothing to scoff at. That sort of attention was getting more and more scant.

Having finished her brief run-down of the evening for Mary and Felicia, Tamara was ready to move on. "Now let's talk about this boy, who he is and what I should do. Between—I mean—*among* the three of us, we should be able to come up with something." Looking at Mary, she asked hopefully, "He's not in your Spanish class is he?"

"No," said Mary, shaking her head.

"He's not in mine either," offered Felicia. "What do you want to happen? I mean do you want to warn them off because they're trespassing? Which, incidentally, you were doing, too, at the time you got bashed."

"I understand why they took off when they hit you in the head; they didn't want to get caught trespassing and probably thought you had a legal right to be there. But why did they take off running the first night you saw them?" Mary wondered out loud.

"I don't know for sure, but I think something scared them," Tamara said. *And it was probably a ghost*, she thought. "And yes," looking at Felicia, "I do want to warn them off. They're talking about some sort of treasure, and the articles I found there were very old, I'm sure. *That house* is old. It's got to be over one hundred forty years old. My parents are trying to find a pre-Civil War cemetery associated with that place. It's supposed to be somewhere in our neighborhood. What if those guys find an artifact that belongs in a museum or, at the very least, to the owners of the house? Nothing there is theirs to take. They need to know they're being watched and that I'm prepared to go to the police."

"The police?" from Felicia.

"My parents, then. They'd know what to do."

"It sounds like you've already decided what to do," Felicia said.

"I'll need your help, Mary," Tamara said, turning back to her.

"How can I help?" Mary asked with a puzzled look. Then, as though a light had come on inside her head, she smiled knowingly and said, "You want me to find out his name from Hank Hanley, don't you?"

"Would you? Please? Then I could look him up in the student directory."

"Sure. I don't mind. Want me to call you or just tell you when I see you in homeroom?"

"Call me. I want to talk to him as soon as I know who he is."

The first period bell ended their conversation. And since Hank wasn't in Mary's Spanish class that day, Tamara didn't get any information until Mary called Wednesday night. The boy's name was Juan Taborga and his number was listed in the student directory. She leaned back against her bed sitting-pillow and thought about what she'd say to him. Should she come on strong or just let him know that she knew who he was? Maybe she should indicate that she'd suffered greatly from the blow to her head, but let him know she wasn't going to press charges. She opted for the straightforward approach and dialed his number. A woman's voice answered, "Bueno."

Wishing she'd signed up for Spanish, Tamara forged ahead. "Hello. Could I please speak to Juan?"

"One moment, please." Thank god she spoke English! Tamara heard her muffled yell. "Juan! Teléfono!" Soon there was a click as Juan picked up an extension.

"Hello?" Another click as his mom, she supposed, hung up.

"Hello, Juan. My name is Tamara. You don't know me, but I live across the street from 1000 Boone. Does that address mean anything to you?"

There was a hesitation before he answered, "No."

"Well, think harder, Juan. Think back to the dark of the night almost two weeks ago when you and your friend trespassed all over that house on Boone. You kept the key, Juan, a key that belongs to the Thompson family." She started getting carried along by her enthusiasm to deter them from returning to the house. Now she wanted to scare him. "You have no right to that key. And you and your friend were there again last Sunday. You left suddenly after hitting me in the head with the kitchen door. I have a huge bruise to show from that collision. Do you remember that, Juan?"

No answer. But he didn't hang up.

"What's your friend's name, Juan?"

"Why are you calling me? What do you want?"

"I want you to stay out of that house—you *and* your friend. And I want the key. That's stolen property."

"I don't have the key."

"Who does?"

No answer.

"Fine, Juan. The only name I have for the police is yours. You can tell *them* who your friend is. I don't need to know."

"No, please! No police!" He was begging now. "I'll get the key for you. Please, no police! We didn't break anything or take anything. We were just looking around."

"I want the key tomorrow at lunch. Do you eat first or second lunch?"

44

"Second, but I don't know if I can get it before lunch tomorrow." He sounded worried. Good!

"Get it, Juan, and meet me in the hall outside the cafeteria *before* second lunch period. I'm easy to recognize. I'll have on a blue baseball cap over the biggest forehead bruise that ever existed."

"Okay, I'll be there. I'll find you. Please swear you won't call the police. We didn't do anything."

"Just return the key tomorrow and everything will be fine, Juan."

"Okay."

"Okay. See you tomorrow outside the cafeteria at 12:30. Good-bye, Juan."

"Okay. Good-bye," he said, hanging up immediately.

Tamara hung up, feeling empowered—and a little like a bully who had just gotten away with intimidation. Maybe she should lay off the *Law and Order* and *NYPD Blue* reruns. She also felt a little sorry for Juan. He sounded like an okay kind of guy. Genius boy was obviously the leader of that duo. She suddenly wondered if he would show up outside the lunchroom, too. She hadn't considered that possibility. Well, so what if he did show? They'd be in a public place. And, anyway, *they* were the trespassers. She was just being a helpful neighbor—in a furtive sort of way.

Tamara switched off her bedside lamp and peered through the dark, across the street to the Thompson house. It was completely dark again tonight, just as it had been every night since she had made that promise to Sarah.

Chapter 7

She picked him out right away. He stood outside the cafeteria door, nervously scanning the hallway full of hungry students. He didn't look the least bit threatening and no one seemed to be accompanying him. He focused on her blue ball cap, then on her as she walked confidently toward him. He kept his eyes on her as she approached and seemed to almost shrink against the wall when she paused in front of him. He was scared.

"Juan?" she asked, looking squarely into his eyes.

"Hi," he managed to say, nodding.

"Did you bring the key?"

Breaking eye contact, he let his eyes follow a student walking past them into the cafeteria. "I couldn't get it from…my friend."

"What you really mean is that he refuses to return it. Am I right?"

Looking at her again, he said, "He doesn't think you have more right to it than he does. I tried really, really hard to convince him to give it to me but he wouldn't." He paused and biting his lower lip, asked, "What are you going to do?"

Not expecting this particular turn of events, Tamara hesitated. Then, gathering her wits together, she asked, "More to the point, Juan, what does *he* intend to do? You two can't keep going into the Thompson house. It's private property and you've been trespassing. It's against the law, Juan." Cocking her head and dropping her upper body slightly, she spoke that last part as though she was addressing a particularly dense person.

"I'm not going there anymore. You're right, we shouldn't be there." Again, there was that hesitation as he bit his lower lip. "But he's right, too. You have no right to be there any more than we do," he said, not looking at her. He spoke so quietly she almost missed it.

"Why are you protecting him, Juan? Don't you understand that eventually this guy is going to get you into trouble? Who is he?" That was a dead end.

Again he asked, "What are you going to do?"

Tamara felt frustrated and didn't know how to answer. She felt protective of the house and of Sarah. Like a ghost *needed* protecting, but still....

"Tell your no-name little friend to stay away from that house. I'll be watching, Juan, and if I see either of you even in the neighborhood, I won't hesitate to call the police. I mean it. Tell him to stay away." Giving him a look that said she meant business, Tamara turned and walked into the cafeteria.

When she reported to Mary and Felicia the next morning, they also wanted to know what she intended to do. "Will you really call the police on a couple of kids," Felicia wanted to know, "or just tell your parents?"

"That really bothers you, doesn't it? Going to the police. That's the second time you've asked me that."

"Well, duh, *yes.*" Felicia added emphasis with the intent look she directed at Tamara. "Calling in the police is serious business, Tamara. You need to give that a lot of thought before going ahead with it. That wouldn't be right. Think about if someone called the police on you. How would you like to have to deal with that? What would your parents say? Think about it a lot, Tamara, before you ever give them a call. Bad shit can happen to a kid and it's really hard to shake afterwards. Police cars outside your house? For all your neighbors to see? Uh-uh, no. The police are serious business. Don't be using their number lightly." Felicia's face flushed darkly when she finished her tirade. But she didn't turn away.

"I think I heard that loud and clear." Tamara felt admonished, but had the wherewithal to take no offense. Instead, she pondered other possibilities for handling the problem of the boys. "Maybe my parents can find out how to get in touch with the owners and let them know that the locks should be changed. They're still working on that cemetery thing, and since that involves the Thompson family, it makes sense that they could find a way to contact them."

"Could be," was all that Felicia had to offer.

Mary, who had witnessed their interchange but had wisely and respectfully remained out of it, now observed, "Correct me if I'm wrong, but you seem unnaturally attached to that old house. Why is that? What's going on that you're not saying out loud?"

This, from Mary—reticent, keep-everything-friendly, nice little middle-class Mary—caught Tamara off guard. What was happening with these two? She felt the bounds of their friendship being stretched. And yet, she didn't want to withdraw from either of them. Mary had hit on the truth, and Felicia kept making her look at herself, her behavior and (*gulp*) her judgments. Even so, the idea of being telekinetically removed to the safety of her room appealed greatly to her at the moment. She looked at Mary, then at Felicia. Both were waiting for her to respond. Tamara risked another step toward honesty with these two. Looking at Mary, "If I promise to tell you later, will you let it go for now?" she asked quietly, her face a study in solemnity.

"When is later?" Mary asked in a like attitude of quiet sobriety.

Tamara was silent for a moment as she deliberated a truthful answer. "When it feels right. That's as close as I can come. But I promise you I *will* answer that. When the time is right."

Mary responded with a silent nodding of her head. And Tamara looked at Felicia, whose face was unreadable but not unfriendly. There was no saving bell to end this awkward moment among them. Felicia, who occupied the lead desk of the trio, turned around and faced forward in her seat. With a glance at Mary behind her, Tamara also faced forward. All three found things to do until first period bell.

None of the three brought up the subject of that anxious moment for the remainder of the week. And although they were able to resume their camaraderie, the necessity of sharing Sarah with them remained an ever-present, eventual duty looming over Tamara. It hung there in her subconscious, making her slightly uncomfortable whenever they were together or when she thought about either of them. Because of that lingering sensation, the end of the school week didn't bring the usual relief for Tamara. A vague, cloudiness hung over her even into Saturday morning, which she spent holed up in her room. The sensation kept her intermittently glancing toward the Thompson house as if *it* could bring her that longed-for relief. The phone had been no help either, ringing for her about six times in two hours. Each call had been a wrong number or, Tamara suspected, possibly a crank caller—some girl or boy she didn't recognize, saying, "Oh, sorry, I must have called the wrong number." She wondered vaguely if the calls had anything to do with Juan or his nameless leader. She eventually gave up trying to accomplish anything substantial in her room—escaping with a book or movie didn't even work out. She *had* to go looking for Sarah, though she felt little hope of finding her. Clicking off her TV, Tamara set out for the Thompson house. Just moving in that direction increased her energy level.

Once inside the old house, where sunlight filled the curtainless kitchen and streamed through the cracks between the living room drapes, Tamara marveled at how comfortable, how welcomed she felt to be there. Her feet seemed to look forward to walking upon the lovely old carpet. Could that be a sign that Sarah would be here this time? She wandered slowly around the perimeter of the living room, prolonging her time there, then through the center, even more slowly. When she reached the door to the dining room, she followed the same ritual, giving Sarah more time to appear. Walking slowly up to the second floor, Tamara started calling quietly to Sarah. Leaving the master bedroom for last, she went through each bedroom looking into closets. Invoking Sarah's name until it became a chant, she circled the room once before approaching the closet. The door was closed just as she had left it last Sunday during her fruitless search for Pearly. Now she reached for the knob and saying, "Sarah, please come back," she turned it and pulled the door open. Before her was just a tiny empty closet. Disappointed, she dropped her hand from the knob and started out of the room. She passed the little circle of sunlight cast by the empty knothole in the closet wall and walked dejectedly down the stairs. Something didn't feel right. Some little intangible something tickled the edges of her consciousness, and she could neither put a name to it nor shake it off.

Tamara wasn't ready to give up and leave, though her mission seemed hopeless. She stared aimlessly around the living room, then went to the window seat left of the fireplace. She plunked herself down and, sighing heavily, leaned her head and back against the fireplace. That position enabled her to see out the gap between the drape and the wall. Striding across the well-tended lawn were two boys her age. One of them was Juan.

Tamara jumped off the window seat and just stood momentarily facing the kitchen. They would be inside in less than a minute. She turned, opened the window seat, stepped in and closed the lid over her before she had time to formulate a clear plan. For now, she did not want them to know she was there.

She hadn't yet arranged her body parts into reasonably comfortable positions when she heard the kitchen door open. She stopped all movement. Listening for any signs of motion in her direction, she remained frozen on hands and knees. There *was* motion in the living room. *She could see it!* Through an almost imperceptible gap between two boards, she could see everything in the living room from the kitchen doorway all the way to the dining room doorway! She hadn't noticed the gap from outside the seat, but there it was. And the boys were headed up the stairs. Had she not been able to see them, she would have no idea of their whereabouts within the house, since the carpet prevented her from hearing their footsteps.

Keeping her eye on the gap between the boards, Tamara counted to sixty. Warily, she opened the window seat lid and looked toward the stairs, listening intently. Though she could make out none of their conversation, she could hear them talking quietly as they wandered around upstairs. Silently, she stepped out of the window seat onto the carpet. They were still moving upstairs and as they walked down the hallway close to the landing, she heard a non-Juan voice say, "This is the biggest room. It must be in here."

"I don't think there's anything here. We should go." *Good old loyal Juan, trying to keep his promise to stay away,* Tamara thought. A light clicked on in her head.

"You're just scared," she heard No-name taunt as she walked into the kitchen. Yes! They had returned the key to its proper place in the door. Trying to turn it to the locked position, she found it was already locked. "I wonder who they were trying to keep out," she mused silently. Smiling to herself, she removed the key to her pants pocket. Still listening for their voices and movements, she moved as quietly as possible into the living room and up the stairs. She prayed a silent thanks to whoever installed this carpet and thought to cover the stairs. Carefully maneuvering the steps, she was aware of the boys quietly arguing their mission. She moved stealthily to the master bedroom door and listened. They continued to argue.

"It's here. I know it is. It's gotta be!"

Counting to three, Tamara took a deep breath and stepped into the doorway. Juan, who was standing outside the closet with his side to the doorway, caught the motion and turned and screamed at the same time. His scream made Tamara scream and brought No-name out of the closet in a hurry. From the look of horror on his face, he was expecting something more ethereal than a mere junior high school girl.

Chapter 8

Having embarrassed herself with her uncontrolled reactionary scream, Tamara made an attempt at feigning righteous indignation. "*What* are you doing here?" She addressed the general direction of the closet.

Juan just stood there woodenly, staring at her, his mouth slightly open. Visibly regaining his composure and drawing himself to his full height, No-name answered arrogantly, "We might ask you the same question—*Tamara.*"

Not knowing Fiddler/Genius/No-name's actual name put Tamara at a definite disadvantage in this battle of wits. Grasping at straws, she let truth take a back seat here and offered, "My parents are working on a research project for this house's owner in order to locate an old cemetery associated with it. I'm keeping an eye out for vandals as a favor to the owner."

Amazingly, her bold-faced lie seemed to have the desired effect on No-name. His control faltered. He was at a loss for words. Seeing her opening, Tamara plunged forward. "So why are you here? What 'treasure' are you looking for?"

Having lost the upper hand, No-name hesitated and appeared to be searching for some answers to appease her. He looked at Juan who was obviously frightened by the possible outcome of this encounter. Tamara feared she had been too hard on the boy. She felt sorry for him again, imagining that she had tortured him with her earlier police threats. Softening and remembering an equalizing technique she had learned in a conflict resolution course in her old school, Tamara indicated the floor in front of them and suggested, "Let's sit down and share some information." Singling out Juan, she said, "Juan, relax. I'm not going to report you to the police. I just want to know what you guys know. And—I'll tell you what I know."

Juan visibly lightened and glanced at No-name as though for permission to do as Tamara had suggested. Tamara made the first move toward settling on the floor and noted with relief that the boys were following her lead. Having founded this triangular convention of cross-legged investigators, Tamara felt obliged to begin. First thing on her agenda was the long overdue answer to the question, "What's your name, anyway? You both know mine and we both," indicating No-name, "know Juan's, but I still don't know your name. What is it?"

"You don't need to know my name in order to get information from me. What do you know about this place? I'll tell you the stories I've heard. They're only stories, old stories, but some people swear they're true and they've been around for so long, I think they must be true." Old No-name was regaining some of his arrogance. Juan was studying his own knees as though he'd never really looked at them before.

Relenting on the name issue, Tamara asked, "So what are the stories? And who told you them?"

"People who have lived around here for a long time. I mean their families have been here since before the Civil War and they know lots of things that happened to all the old families. You know—historical stuff. Anyway, some kids I know have been telling me these stories about a lost treasure of thousands of dollars. It's money that's been missing since the old guy who built this house died during the Civil War. He was murdered—supposedly." He paused as though expecting something from Tamara. When she didn't respond, he shrugged his shoulders and said, "That's it, basically. Somewhere in the house there's supposed to be a lot of hidden money."

The hair on the back of Tamara's neck had begun to stand up at the mention of "the old guy…died during the Civil War. He was murdered…." This boy was telling Sarah's story, the story of her father, from another perspective—his, a purely historical perspective—gleaned from the telling and re-telling of generations of Benjamin Thompson's neighbors. He was offering unbidden validation of a tale told to her by a ghost. *Sarah's story was true.* The incidents she had recounted had really occurred—in another lifetime.

"Hey! I said, 'That's it.' Come on!" Tamara was brought out of her reverie by No-name's rude expression of impatience.

"Are you sure that's all?" she asked, not knowing in what direction to take this conversation.

"Well, everyone who talks about it also says the house has been haunted for over forty years. Hardly anyone has lived here for all that time. People who moved in, moved out soon afterward because of the ghost." He paused again, briefly, then asked, "So what do you know?"

Unsure of whether or not to disclose the "treasure" she had found, Tamara hesitated.

"Hey, we had a deal here. I told my part. What do you know?" His arrogance had really regained its foothold. Obligated by a sense of fair play, Tamara would have to tell him what she had found in the window seats. As she deliberated just how to proceed, she became aware of a sudden temperature drop in the sunny room. Encouraged by the cold air and what it must mean, she began her tale of hidden treasure.

"I found some things that I think are important historically. And, yes, they're probably worth a lot of money." The room was growing colder by the minute and she knew they felt it, too. Juan had stopped examining his knees and crossed his arms in an effort to contain his body heat. No-name pulled on the jacket he had been carrying over his arm. "But they belong in a museum. None of us has the right to even touch them until they've been examined by experts. *Archeological* experts." The cold in the room was deepening. Tamara considered it a sign from Sarah that she was on the right track. She quickly formulated a plan and began to proceed with it. "What you might find even more interesting than those *things* is what led me to them. Or should I say who?" Tamara was enjoying taking No-name on this little journey now. If Juan got singed in the process, maybe he'd learn to hang with a better class of friends. How could the cold be increasing? Tamara was starting to feel really uncomfortable with the chilled air. And the boys? She expected to see them patting their arms from cold any minute now. "You see, guys, when I found the 'treasure,' I was on a quest for a little friend who I met up here one night. I think you might have met her, too." Juan seemed to be listening now. His face grew wary. No-name appeared to be busy with staying warm. Neither boy interrupted her story by responding to her suggestion. "On your first night here? When you went flying from the house as though you'd seen a...ghost?" No-name looked up now and both boys looked with horror-stricken faces past Tamara to the doorway. Smugly, Tamara continued, "Let me introduce you. Juan, No-name, may I present Sarah Thompson?" She turned from her sitting position, with a flourish of her arm and twist of her wrist, pointing all fingers of her upturned palm toward the door where she was certain she would find little Sarah was standing. When her eyes fell upon denim-covered legs, attached to an adult woman towering over their conference, Tamara screamed for the second time that afternoon.

Chapter 9

The face of the woman in the doorway had taken on a questioning look of surprise as Tamara's hand had swept toward her. Seconds later she stepped backward as though jarred by Tamara's scream before her face regained its composure and she spoke.

"Well, you seem to know who I am. Now I'd like to know who each of you are and what you're doing here."

Her demeanor and even tone carried a clear expectation of their compliance. But before any of them could make up an answer, they were distracted by heavy pounding on the front door, followed by, "Police! We're here to investigate a reported illegal entry."

"Stay put," the woman ordered before disappearing down the stairs. All three were silent while she was gone. Tamara, imagining her parents' reaction to her involvement in this situation, was not so preoccupied that she missed how Juan's face had grown dark with anxiety and he was chewing a corner of his lower lip again, as he had at their first meeting. No-name rubbed the knuckles of one hand over and over the middle of his bottom lip. The three had found a common bond—fear.

When the woman reappeared at the top of the stairs she found them just as she had left them. She looked at each of their faces, then said, "Oh my god, cheer up! I've sent the police away." She paused briefly. "But not that far away, so don't get any wild ideas. The doors are locked and I've got the key. By the way, I'll accept the return of the kitchen key without judgment."

With one hand on her hip, she extended the other, palm up, in their direction. Realizing her compromised position, Tamara reached into her pocket and, extending the key to the proffered hand, her face begging for understanding, she began, "I only took it to...."

"No judgment, remember?" the woman interrupted, shaking her head and holding up a hand to ward off Tamara's excuse. "Okay, everyone up," she said with an authority that brooked no refusal. "We're going downstairs for a little party. I don't know about you guys, but all this excitement has made me hungry. And, lucky you," she said with feigned joviality, "I've brought snacks enough to share. Let's go!"

The three rose as one and started down the stairs. The woman followed. "Make yourselves useful. Head for the kitchen."

Once there she began instructing them in the unloading of two grocery bags resting on the counter. Upon entering the kitchen, No-name came out of his trance to say, "I can't stay. My mom's expecting me home in fifteen minutes."

"I can fix that. What's her number? I've brought my cell phone just for such emergencies." She had removed a phone from her back pocket as she spoke and was opening it. "And what's her name?"

"Never mind. I'll explain to her later."

"I just bet you will," she responded before resuming instructions on their picnic preparations.

"Excuse me," interrupted Juan, "but I need to call my house and let them know where I am."

"Yeah, me, too," Tamara chimed in, glad that Juan had made that move and she wouldn't have to bring it up. This woman *was* a stranger, after all, no matter how benevolent she seemed regarding lunch and the police.

"Good move, you two. I was beginning to wonder at your upbringing, but I see your parents have instructed you well regarding strangers. You're pretty brave kids considering that you're trespassing on my property. But let's not dwell on that for the moment." She handed her phone to Juan and turned to No-name. "You'd better call home, too. I'm certain you can think of *something* to tell your mom."

With calls home completed and the food prepared and divided on paper plates, they all retired to the living room, since there was no place to sit in the kitchen. From the amount of food and paper accoutrements, it appeared that the woman had been expecting company or intended to stay for more than an afternoon. When all were seated on the window seats, she dove eagerly into her tuna sandwich. Watching her, the kids followed suit. Surprised to find that she was indeed extremely hungry, Tamara was grateful for the unexpected food. The boys, too, eagerly partook of chips and veggies to round out their meal. Eating sounds were all that was heard until the woman swallowed, cleared her throat and, zooming in on Tamara, asked, "So how did you know my name?"

Her mouth full of sandwich, Tamara cocked her head and shook it. With a bewildered look, she denied the premise of the woman's question. "I don't know your name," she said when she was able to speak.

"But you…" the woman began. Then as if she could find the answer to her puzzlement there, she stared into the pattern of the carpet at her feet. Her face changed to a look of someone gaining a slowly dawning, barely credible, possible solution. Looking back up at Tamara, she asked, "Who were you expecting?" Tamara's sudden flush and ducking of her head seemed to encourage the woman's line of thinking. "Were you expecting a child?" When Tamara didn't answer, she asked, "A ghost, perhaps?"

Confronted with such direct questions, Tamara's discomfort with the notion of communicating with a ghost overwhelmed her. She felt trapped. Her secret was about to come out and she felt exposed and foolish. A hand touching her knee surprised her. The woman, with a total change from her wise-guy demeanor, was speaking in a gentle, comforting voice. "It's alright. Other people have seen her. I believe *I* saw her, though barely, on my way up the stairs today. It was almost as though she was rushing past me to get to the top first."

All chewing and crunching had stopped. "We saw a candle that first night." The voice was Juan's. As he continued, he appeared to weigh each word before speaking it aloud. "It was just—floating—in the air— at the top of the stairs."

Tamara breathed a deep sigh and looking up at the woman said, "Yes. I thought it would be her—not you. The air got all cold like it did when she was around."

"Yeah!" both boys chimed in at once.

"I noticed it, too, as I walked up the stairway." The woman looked around at them. She seemed to be making a decision about how to continue based on what she read in their faces. "Let's start at the usual starting place with introductions all around. I'm Sarah Thompson and this house is mine. It has been since last spring." She turned to Tamara sitting on her left. Tamara, her face enveloped in a look of confusion, stared back at her.

"But you're..." Tamara struggled for the right adjective. "You're real."

Smiling broadly, as she comprehended the source of Tamara's confusion, big Sarah Thompson said, "Oh yes, very, though I believe I was named after your friend the ghost."

"Oohh," Tamara sighed, smiling with relief and falling back against the fireplace, as understanding dawned. "That makes sense. Of course, you're *named after her*. She's your grandmother?"

"Great-great-aunt. And your name is?"

"Oh, sorry! I'm Tamara Burns."

"Juan Taborga," Juan said when she looked his way.

"You don't need to know my name," was No-name's arrogant response when she directed her attention toward him.

Picking up her cell phone and pressing the on/off switch, Big Sarah said, with obvious irritation, "No, kiddo, I don't need to get it from you. But I bet your mother would be able to tell me with less attitude. Let's see. Weren't you the last person to place a call on my phone?" she asked, pretending ignorance of the answer. Then with a self-satisfied smirk, addressing them all, she continued. "Cell phones and all their functions come in so handy at times. You know if you want to call back the last person you talked to, you don't have to know or look up their number. You can just press 'talk' and the phone dials it automatically." She pressed the talk button as she spoke and put the phone to her ear.

"No, don't!" No-name yelled, his arrogance going dormant again. "I'm Jake. Please don't call my mom."

"Good decision, Jake," she said, canceling the call. "I didn't catch that last name, though."

Eyeing the phone in her hand, "Greenleaf," he said, quietly.

Turning off the phone and putting it down, Sarah looked around at them again and asked, "Shall we try to keep this friendly and start again, Tamara, Juan and Jake? Why are we all here? I can begin." And without waiting, she did. "My neighbors have been calling me for weeks about suspicious activity in this house. It's taken me this long to find time to check out their reports. I notified the police that I was on my way over here after the call I received earlier today. I was actually packing up to spend the evening here when I got that last call." She paused, then finished with, "So there you have my story. What's yours?" Turning to Jake, she said, "You've been so reticent, Jake. Let's hear from you first."

"We were talking about that just before you showed up," he began agreeably. "I was telling Tamara that some friends of mine, whose family has lived around here since before the Civil War, swear that there's treasure hidden in this house. It belonged to the old guy who built the house. He was murdered and no one ever found the money he stashed. But I guess you must already know that since you're related to him. My cousin and I were just taking a look around to see if there was any truth to the story."

"Cousin? Juan, you two are cousins?" Tamara asked as though Jake wasn't a reliable source. When Juan, his face drawn down into a frown, answered by nodding his head, Tamara decided she had misjudged the poor kid, cousins not being a matter of choice.

Ignoring Tamara's interruption, Sarah asked Jake, "And did you find anything?"

"No. That first night we saw the floating candle and didn't stick around."

"*I'll say they didn't!*" Feeling that Jake was downplaying and abridging his story, Tamara again broke into his telling of it. "And the next time, they opened the kitchen door just as I was leaving and hit me in the head with it," she eagerly volunteered.

"And what were you doing here?" Sarah asked.

Tamara started to answer, then stopped, realizing that in Big Sarah's eyes, she had no legitimate reason for being in the house. Before she could string together the right words to explain her position, Jake jumped in with, "She told *us* that she was watching this house as a favor to you!"

"Hey, yeah! She said you and her parents were researching your family cemetery!" Juan interjected. Shifting his focus back to Tamara, he added accusingly, "And, Tamara, she didn't even know who you were until you just told her! You made that stuff up!"

Tamara was embarrassed to be caught in a lie and singled out for disfavor in front of an adult. But unwilling to become their scapegoat and needing her behavior judged in a more favorable light, she defended herself. "I only *intimated* that I was acting with your permission," she said, directing her defense toward Sarah. "And my parents really *are* engrossed in locating a family cemetery associated with this house. They've been working on it for weeks. Getting in touch with the owner of this house has to be on their list of things to do. I'm sure you'll be hearing from them any day now. They're archeologists. Maybe they've called you already?" Losing steam, she ended lamely.

"Are you trying to convince me that your being in this house the day you collided with the door had to do with your parents' project?"

Interpreting the woman's mood to be one of no tolerance for anything less than the absolute truth, Tamara answered, "No, I'm not saying that. I was saying that to *them*," indicating Juan and Jake with a toss of her head in their direction, "earlier, when I wanted them to take me seriously. But the reason I was here that other day was because Sarah, the other Sarah, asked me..." self-consciously she looked away at nothing, then back at Big Sarah, before finishing, "to find her doll for her."

And beginning at the beginning, with her first sighting of the dim, flickering light in the upstairs window, Tamara recounted, aloud for the first time, the entire story. The tale of her relationship with Little Sarah (as Tamara had come to think of her since the advent of Big Sarah to the Thompson house) took precedence over finishing their meal. Her audience remained quiet and attentive throughout her tale. When she got to the discovery within the window seats, Big Sarah interrupted her and shooed the three of them off the seats in order to inspect the artifacts Tamara had described. Upon opening the one to the left of the fireplace, Big Sarah's interest was drawn to the quilt. She touched it tentatively and, kneeling in order to bring her face close to it without removing the quilt from the window seat, she looked at it almost reverently.

"It's the monkey-wrench pattern," she said quietly. Then turning to look at the adolescents at her elbows, she asked, "Are you familiar with it? Do you know what it means?" When they shook their heads or otherwise indicated a negative answer to her question, she turned back to the quilt. A new mood had settled over her. There was a holy-temple-reverence air to her actions now. None of them spoke or even moved until Big Sarah turned to Tamara. "Show me the panel now."

Moving to the fireplace end of the window seat, Tamara bent down and pushed on the bottom of the panel, exposing the secret cell. She moved out of the way so that Big Sarah could look closely at its contents. Doing so without reaching into the recess, Big Sarah shook her head slowly. "This is remarkable," she said to all three of them. "It's just remarkable! I had no idea this house was anything more than a renovation project." Moving into a more enlivened state, she instructed Tamara, "Show me the other panel." Tamara complied and when it too had been inspected and the window seats closed, Big Sarah sat contemplatively atop the one to the right of the fireplace. Jake broke into her preoccupation.

"What are you going to do with those things?" he asked brusquely.

Looking up from her reverie, she answered slowly. "I guess I'm going to call the University. Someone who knows more than I do needs to see this stuff. But I'm really struck by the quilt. I read something about that particular pattern at an exhibit at the folk museum a couple of weeks ago. It's called the monkey wrench and is thought to have been a signal of some sort to pre-Civil War slaves—maybe a message for people planning their escape to the north." She shrugged her shoulders. "I don't know what the other items are—a lantern, maybe and a money purse, I think. I don't know what the other thing could be." Directing her gaze to Tamara, she said, "That's quite a tale you've related, Tamara. Why do you suppose she's chosen *you?*" Without waiting for Tamara to answer, she asked, "Is there more to your story?"

"I searched the whole house thoroughly and couldn't find anything, except what you just saw in the window seats. There's nothing else— not even any broken windows or clutter. I couldn't find any places where anything could be lost," Tamara said. Turning toward Jake, she added, "Or hidden."

Jake threw Tamara a sarcastic smile and turning to Big Sarah asked, with a resurgence of his old arrogance, "Are we finished here, now? Can I go?"

Juan hung back. "I haven't told my part yet," he told Jake. "I'm going to stay awhile. And I'll help clean up," he said, brandishing a hand toward the remains of their lunch. His enthusiasm for staying behind earned him a roll of Jake's eyes and a groan. Big Sarah escorted Jake out the front door, assuring him with a hint, in equal measures, of sarcasm and intimidation that she would "be keeping in touch."

Tamara, ruminating through her Thompson house experiences of the past two weeks, culminating in this afternoon's adventure, paid little attention to Jake's exit. She was experiencing a return of the unease she had felt at other times within the house. Some things were wrong, didn't make sense and she couldn't pin them down, couldn't even identify a category for the feeling.

Rejoining the quiet twosome at the fireplace, Big Sarah spoke to Tamara. "I sense there's more to be told. You ended your story with your window seat discoveries. There has to be some transition from that to the scene I walked in upon—the three of you sitting in a circle on the floor. How'd you get from here to that mutual admiration society upstairs?" Her tongue-in-cheek air was back.

"Hey, good question! How did you? We waited until we knew you weren't home before we came over. Then Jake locked the door after we came in—particularly so that you *couldn't* get in!" Juan had grown more animated this afternoon than at any other time Tamara had seen him.

"So who'd you get to make those wrong-number calls?"

"You knew about that?" he asked, incredulous.

"I do now."

Blushing, embarrassed that she had so easily entrapped him, Juan still wanted to know, "How did you get in? The door was locked."

"I was already inside. I saw the two of you coming across the yard and I hid in that window seat," Tamara answered, pointing to it. "I watched you go upstairs and waited until…oh my god! Juan, *I watched you go upstairs!*" Tamara's excitement was growing out of bounds quickly. She almost grabbed Juan to make him understand. Seeing the clueless look on his face she turned instead to Big Sarah. "Sarah, get it? I *saw* them! I saw *everything* from that doorway to that one!" Tamara was gesticulating wildly now. She stepped in front of the left window seat, leaving nearly five feet of space between it and herself. Looking back at her more sedate and very confused companions, she threw her arms out, palms up, as though she was presenting the window seat to them. "Look! Do you see a gap? I don't." Not waiting for them to be struck by her light, she brushed past them, yanked open the window seat to the right and climbed in on all fours. With her face almost pressed against the inside of the box, she called up to them, "Same here!" Tamara bopped up to a kneeling position. Smiling, more excited than before— if possible—she said, "I can see everything from this one, too!" She scrambled out of the box. The light suddenly illuminating Tamara's vision had yet to pierce the darkness for either of the other two. "Don't you get it? I'm *supposed* to see everything! *Sarah*, people waited in there for a chance to escape! *They hid slaves in this house!*" Tamara nearly yelled into Big Sarah's face, she was so excited!

Dawn was just approaching for Juan and Big Sarah when Tamara received her second epiphany. "Sarah's closet! It must be hidden, too!" she explained excitedly. Tamara ran up the stairs into the master bedroom closet. She studied its three little walls and its ceiling for some clue, some sign of a hiding place. Frustrated, she backed quickly out of the closet, nearly stepping on Big Sarah. Distractedly mumbling an apology, she practically raced into the adjacent bedroom and inspected the closet there. Disappointed, her frustration growing, she returned more slowly to the master bedroom. With her eyes cast down she entered the doorway. Big Sarah and Juan were waiting for her in the middle of the room. Disappointment written all over her face and in her carriage, Tamara was about to explain the apparently erroneous hypothesis accounting for her former excitement, when she passed and obliterated the small circle of sunlight focused upon the wall by the empty knothole. She took a couple of steps backward in order to see it reappear. Then, wearing a puzzled expression, she walked into the closet and looked up at the hole above her head. Still puzzled and repeating, "There has to be a hidden closet here," she hurried back into the next bedroom and carefully examined the wall separating the two rooms. Once again she returned to the master bedroom closet and tried, unsuccessfully, to poke her finger up into the knothole. She glanced slowly around the room as though she was looking for something on the floor. Turning to the middle of the room, she asked, "Do either of you have a pen or pencil on you? Or anything small enough to go into this knothole?"

"I have a pocket knife. Maybe one of the blades or the hole punch will be small enough," Big Sarah offered, reaching into a jeans pocket and pulling out a multi-bladed Swiss Army knife. Tamara accepted it with thanks and gently poked the smallest blade through the knothole. "There's empty space on the other side of this wall, but I didn't see any hole when I was just in the next room. Can one of you go into the other closet and see if you can see the knife blade?"

"I will," said Juan hurrying out of the room. "I can't see anything," he called shortly from the next room.

"Okay, thanks!" she yelled back and turned to face Sarah. "I think that means there's some kind of space between this closet wall and the wall of the next room. There has to be. There has to be a windowed room because there's enough light coming through to make that circle of light on the wall there. But I can't figure out how to get to it." While talking to Big Sarah, she began feeling and pushing against the back wall to no avail. Then she felt and pushed against the right wall, again with no success. Nor did the left wall reveal any secret doors or latches to her searching fingers. Frustrated, feeling thwarted on every hand, she glanced over her shoulder, only to see Big Sarah and Juan standing next to each other in the center of the room staring at her with similar worried looks on their faces.

Taking a step toward Tamara, Big Sarah said, "Tamara, I can see that you're invested in helping Sarah. And maybe your thinking is right. Maybe a hidden room once existed. But who's to say it wasn't turned into a closet or used to expand a bedroom by another resident down the line? And maybe the window seats are all the hidden spaces there ever were in this house."

"No, it *has* to be here! I know that now. It has to!" she insisted. "Look at the light on the wall!" Tamara pointed. "Where is it coming from?"

Irritated at their lack of understanding, because it only accentuated her own prior failure to fully comprehend Little Sarah's story, Tamara turned back to the closet more determined than ever to find something proving she hadn't lost her sanity. With one hand on either side of the vertical timber, which supported the closet's horizontal pole, she searched the wooden beam in one fluid downward movement, again to no avail. Angry at this defeat, she brought both hands back up the timber all the way to the top in a motion that was both too fast and too forceful. Her forefingers on each hand struck the wooden crosspiece atop the upright beam at the same time, pushing it upward an inch or so. When the crosspiece moved up, the right wall of the closet moved slightly away from Tamara. She was so shocked to suddenly find the thing for which she had been so desperately searching that she just gasped and crumpled against the left closet wall, unable to speak, gesturing and staring up at Big Sarah and Juan, both now crowded into the closet doorway. Seeing Tamara's distress, Big Sarah reached into the closet for Tamara's hand and held it in both of hers. She nodded to Juan, who stretched one arm into the closet in front of them and pushed on the wall, standing slightly ajar, until it stood open at a ninety-degree angle. The three of them stared into a long, narrow room, equipped along the left side with two sets of sturdy triple-tiered shelves or, perhaps, bunks. Its floor, walls and ceiling were covered with carpeting identical to that in the living room and on the stairs. An elaborate, two-story dollhouse sat against the right wall halfway into the room. A half-burned candle, still ensconced in its holder, lay on the floor in front of it. But Tamara's eyes were riveted to the antique doll lying on the end of the bottom bunk nearest the door. Lots of white petticoat showed, since the skirt of its blue dress was awry and folded back against a large part of the bodice, but not so much as to cover the topmost, white, real pearl button.

Chapter 10

May 17, 1863

I believe Corey is watching my family's every move and am heartened that all is in place to resettle Annie and Sarah in Canada for the remainder of this wretched war. Please, God, let it be over soon! There is no reason to wait beyond tomorrow and I have informed Annie so. I know it will be trying for all of us. Perhaps more so for Thomas and myself than for either Annie or Sarah. For all the noise we men make about the limitations of the fairer sex, I fear we are only consoling ourselves for how little they actually require of our services in their daily lives. On the other hand, I believe both Thomas and I would starve to death in less than a fortnight after Annie's departure, were it not for the hotel restaurant and Philomena's café. But even with my appetite appeased, I will miss them sorely. What will life be like without them? This house will be too quiet without Sarah's endless questions. Thomas will miss her as well. No one could fail to see the change that comes over him when Sarah enters the room and races into his arms. His face fairly lights up. He loves his little sister more than I could have imagined possible with such a span of years between them. His mother must look down upon him with pride.

This morning I will ride to the Emerson farm and choose that kitten with fur of many shades of grey, the one Sarah has been calling Grace ever since she heard me remark to Wesley that her coat contained so many different greys. I trust that kitten will provide her with a constant and enjoyable focus during their long journey. I will take the balsa cage with me this morning. The trip back will be a good test of whether my design is good and the balsa strong enough. I keep imagining the look of surprise on Sarah's face when I bring it home.

She has been pestering me so while I have been writing this morning! I made the mistake of mentioning I was going to see Josh after breakfast and now she wants to go with me to see the kittens. But I feel the need to act with ever greater caution in public these days as Corey's anger towards me and my family seems to have increased since Mr. Lincoln's proclamation in January. Corey and his following of cowards might find Sarah easy prey on the road to Emerson's farm. I still believe that band of self-righteous thugs is responsible for the deaths of Mary's Theo and the Singletons' Ruth. So I have promised her a secret surprise that she can play with while I am gone. The dollhouse I intended for her seventh birthday will have to be brought out of hiding. There will be no room for that dollhouse on the wagon to Canada. She might as well get some pleasure from it now, since it could be a considerable amount of time before this town becomes safe enough for their return. I am not ready to tell Annie or Thomas about the secret room. Their safety could still be jeopardized by the knowledge of it. I just feel better that they could not unintentionally alert any of our many pro-slavery fanatics to its existence. Sarah will not be a danger in that way because she is a child who knows the value of secrets. And she is leaving tomorrow. She is so young, I feel sure she will have forgotten about it by the time she returns. And in any case, there should never again be need for such rooms when the war is finished. However, I intend to make sure she knows the importance of being very quiet while playing there. I think she will like it immensely! Annie will think Sarah has gone with me to the Emerson place. I shall leave off writing about it now and fetch the kitten when Sarah is safely involved in play behind the closet.

Chapter 11

Tamara was nervous. They would be here any minute. So much had happened in so short of a time, it was hard to know where to begin. Would they believe her? Think she was crazy? She did have evidence and backup support from Big Sarah and Juan if necessary. But it would be great if they didn't require more than her say-so. More than anything she wanted that from her friends today.

She heard their laughter coming from the sidewalk below her open window. Jumping off her bed, she leaned into the screen and yelled down to them. "The door's open. Come up."

"Hey."

"Okay. We're on our way."

Tamara jumped back on the bed and pulled out a pillow to hug against her chest while she waited.

"What's happening across the street?" Mary wanted to know as soon as she got through the bedroom door.

"Isn't that the house you and the boys have been checking out?" Felicia asked.

"Uh-huh. The University sent some people over to check out those things I told you about. And some other stuff."

"No kidding! Tamara, that's so cool! You could be a celebrity!" Mary was beside herself with excitement.

"Or go to jail," Felicia offered with an impish grin.

"Very funny. I'll die laughing later if it's all the same to you." Indicating the bed, Tamara continued so that she would not be able to back out of her resolve, "Sit down and be serious." Obediently they sat and Tamara began. "I said I'd tell you the whole story when the time was right and I think it is. Right, that is, right now. Thanks, by the way. I really needed for you both to be here and I didn't give you much notice. So I appreciate your coming."

"No big deal," said Felicia.

"I'm all ears with a lead-in like that," Mary quipped.

Still anxious in anticipation of their response, Tamara hugged her pillow more tightly to her chest and, looking down into the bedspread between her feet, she started. "When I told you about seeing a light at the Thompsons', I let you think it was the guys' flashlights. It wasn't. For a couple of weeks I had been seeing a tiny, dim light in one of the upstairs windows. When I went over the first night, it was because of that little upstairs light—flickering, like a candle—and when I got back here to my room, the light was still there. And it was there again on that Friday night after dinner. So I went over to check it out."

Tamara took a deep breath and exhaled forcefully. She looked at her friends' faces. They were open and sober. Her chest felt tight as she made herself continue. "I'm completely serious. This is true and exactly what happened." She paused only for an instant, while she decided how to open into the ghost part. "I didn't know it then but that house's been haunted for years. That's why it's empty. No one wanted to live with a ghost. Well, I saw her—the ghost. She's a little girl, six years old, from the Civil War. She talked to me, told me her father had told her to wait in the closet and other stuff. She had a candle in a candleholder. I touched her. She seemed real—spooky or something, but real. But she wasn't. And I haven't seen her since that night. And I was looking for her doll, Pearly, not for treasure, when I got hit in the head by the door." Again Tamara breathed in deeply, exhaled heavily, then searched her friends' faces as she awaited their responses. Both girls' eyes had grown large during her recital.

"A real ghost? How could you tell?" from Felicia.

"What exactly did she say? Were you scared? Where'd she go? Did she fade away while you watched?" from Mary.

Relieved by their excited questioning-but-not-disbelieving reactions, Tamara answered their questions and filled in all the holes in her story. Now that she could relax in the comfort of her friends' trust, the whole story rolled off her tongue and she brought them up to date on the goings-on at the Thompson house. Life was good, very good.

Chapter 12

The opening coincided with the first day of spring. Sunday afternoon promised to be a beautiful, sunny day, after five days of fierce rain and wind. Tamara awoke excited at the prospect of the day before her, and yet there was that troubling, unfinished feeling hanging on, hanging over her. Little Sarah had never revisited her. Sometimes Tamara felt as though she had made Sarah up. After all, there had been only that one night that they had spoken—a long night, true, but only one, just six months ago, and it seemed ages had passed. So many things had happened in her life. The biggest thing was her friendship with Mary and Felicia. The three of them had become practically inseparable. Tamara had never had friendships like the ones she shared with each of them. It made her smile to herself as she started her day, smile in spite of that sad, unfinished, hanging-on feeling.

As one o'clock neared, Tamara walked out to the sidewalk to meet Felicia and Mary for the Thompson House opening activities and tour. Cars and people were beginning to congregate on their once quiet little street. Tamara winced as she considered for the first time those unwelcome changes to her life as she knew it, as she had come to expect it. Well, at least for now, the tours would only be happening on weekend afternoons. And the whole thing *was* exciting. Her involvement in the discoveries within the Thompson House and her parents' continuing association with the museum and cemetery had brought her somewhat of a celebrity status at school and in history class in particular. As a matter of fact, history had turned into her favorite, most looked-forward-to class in the last six months. It was suddenly fun to learn as much as possible about Maryland history. She had even written some English papers on pre-Civil War Maryland, spending hours, weekends in the library doing research.

Felicia and Mary turned the corner onto Tamara's street and waved greetings in her direction. Tamara's stomach tightened with anticipation, as though she was about to begin a performance of some sort—and she wasn't. They were going to be a part of the tour along with everyone else. That was all. But it made her feel celebrated that her friends wanted to be there with her for the first tour.

"Guess who's coming? Juan! We saw him riding in a carful of kids back there," Mary called out as they got closer.

"Juan's okay," said Tamara. "I kind of like him. He grows on you after a while."

"I think he's kind of cute," Mary returned.

"What*ever*," Felicia and Tamara responded in unison, rolling their eyes.

"*He is!*" Mary insisted.

"Let's go on over," Tamara said, changing the subject. "I think Sarah will start things on time. She was really excited last night. And very happy with all the restoration details. Her friend Jennifer is going to do the opening speech."

They talked as they moved with the growing crowd toward the Thompson House.

"My dad's coming by later for a tour. He's rounding up a bunch of his friends to drag down here. He's very proud, Tamara," Felicia said, smiling. Then she added, "And so am I."

"Wow, thanks, Felicia," Tamara returned, genuinely touched.

"Me, too, Tamara. All this is happening because of you. You should be getting some kind of permanent credit at the museum."

"Thanks, Mary," Tamara said. And though she was warmed by her friends' obvious pride in her, her smile was perfunctory. After a pause, she said with a sigh, "I can't stop thinking about Little Sarah. She's the real person, so to speak, responsible for all the discoveries. And she hasn't gotten *anything*. We found her doll, but so what? I mean that's neat; the doll's cool and everything, but is Sarah satisfied? What have I *done* for her?"

"Somehow I think she knows and appreciates you," Mary offered.

"That's not it. I want to know that she's happy, resting easy now. If she never comes back, I'll never know for sure."

The street had become thick with people now and from somewhere up ahead a child demanded, "Pick me up, Mama! I can't see!"

"Carry her on your shoulders, Tom. Would you please?"

The back of a child's head suddenly bobbed among the crowd of adult heads as the demanding child was lifted to someone's shoulders.

"There are a lot of people here, Tamara," Mary said, continuing their conversation as they followed the teeming masses, now crushing Sarah Thompson's newly manicured lawn. "Maybe she needs things to settle down a little before she feels all right about contacting you again."

"I guess," Tamara replied, remaining unencouraged.

"Hey, cool! I didn't know there were going to be any re-enactments today. Did you see those people in Civil War-looking clothes?" a woman, squeezing past Felicia, asked of her companion.

"They must be professional actors. They seem so comfortable in their costumes," he replied.

Catching their bit of conversation, "I guess Big Sarah didn't fill me in on everything about today's happenings," Tamara said to her friends.

Once inside the museum, the crowd had to be broken down into groups of ten. Tamara, Felicia and Mary were in the third tour group so they had plenty of time to admire the renovation work and go through brochures. The Thompson House was slated to become part of an eventual statewide Underground Railroad historic tour. For the opening the Maryland Museum of African American History and Culture had sent over an array of pamphlets regarding other related sites and topics. One brochure gave a historical outline of the Underground Railroad in the United States and a brief history of the secret organization in Maryland. It named and mapped other sites that were once on routes to freedom throughout the state. Another explained the reputed uses of quilt designs to aid escaping slaves. Still another described the Banneker-Douglass Museum in Annapolis. The three girls became engrossed in the reading materials but were ready to begin when Jennifer greeted their group and began her tour spiel.

"Thanks for coming to the Thompson House opening day. My name is Jennifer Mettenburg and I'm here to provide information regarding this house and the slavery era people who lived here. Research is still being conducted regarding the existence of a cemetery plot holding the remains of some of the Thompson family." At the mention of the cemetery, both Felicia and Mary, wearing big smiles, elbowed Tamara who was sandwiched between them. "When the cemetery is located, we hope it will become part of the Thompson House tour. For today, the tour will include the house and grounds currently owned by Sarah Thompson, a descendant of the original residents. If you have any questions, please hold onto them until I've completed the history of the house and its family. The Thompson story has been put together from newspaper archives and journals kept by Benjamin, Rebecca, Annie and Thomas Thompson, as well as the diary of Catherine Corey." She paused as she looked the group over. Then she added, "And from the tale told by a ghost-child of her experiences within these walls." Again, Tamara was pummeled with the elbows of her two smilingly proud sidekicks. Jennifer paused again to let her words sink in with the group before continuing.

"This house, designed by Benjamin Thompson, a renowned architect in this area, was built in 1839. Mr. Thompson actually did some of the building himself. He did so because his wife, Rebecca Louise Talbot Thompson, and he intended from the beginning of their marriage to be stationmasters on the Underground Railroad. In an effort to keep secret hiding places known only to the two of them, he completed the building of the master bedroom, the skylight and the window seats you can see on either side of the fireplace.

"As you will see when you tour the second floor, the master bedroom held a very small closet, hiding a secret room. Over two hundred escaping slaves stayed there until they could be safely transported or escorted to the next safe house on the long road to Canada and freedom. Some parts of the Thompson family story that you'll hear today have come from the recent discovery of Benjamin Thompson's diaries, hidden for one hundred forty years behind his bedroom closet.

"That windowless room was lighted by means of a skylight developed and installed by Benjamin Thompson. Since a skylight could be noticed from outside the house, Benjamin concocted a scheme to account for its structure upon the roof. The skylight's design was based upon those used on seaworthy ships, that is, basically, a windowed tube extending from the roof to the ceiling of the interior room to be lighted. He talked up his skylight as though it was to be used to light the living room, the room in which we're standing. In reality he intended it to be the only source of light for the secret room on the second floor. Benjamin had to present his invention to the public as a failure, as though an error in his design prevented it from providing natural light to this room. Of course, it could never deliver light to the living room since the light tube never extended beyond the ceiling of the second floor. However, it did its real job of lighting the hidden room very well during the daytime. The room was seldom lighted at night. Whoever resided there during darkness was expected to rest for their long journey or be waiting for an escort to move them safely to their next station. Benjamin covered the living room's fake skylight hole and hung an elaborate chandelier, much like the one you see there now. This one was placed there during the recent restoration, since in the intervening years, an electric fixture had replaced candles and kerosene as a means of lighting the house.

"If you come with me to the window seat on the left of the fireplace, you'll see that there's enough room to hide an adult inside there." When the group had moved to the window seat, Jennifer continued. "A push against the bottom of this end panel reveals a hidden compartment." She demonstrated. "Stashed within this compartment were a compact lantern fueled probably with olive oil, a change purse with enough money to enable a runaway to purchase food during his or her flight and a map, disguised as a quilt piece, of the route to be followed. Feel free to carefully inspect either window seat and the compartment near the fireplace. They've been built so that the person within can see out into the room, but anyone standing outside the boxes can't see into them while the seat is down." As members of the tour group examined the window seats and tested the secret panels, Jennifer continued her narrative.

"Benjamin and Rebecca were married for fifteen years. During that period they hid two hundred forty-three runaways from slavery, some from the immediate area, others passing through Maryland from Florida and Georgia. No one else in the household was privy to information regarding their Underground Railroad involvement or the hiding places within the house. No one. The Thompsons felt that total secrecy was imperative to protect those fleeing from slavery as well as those who remained behind.

"The Thompsons were Quakers. Rebecca had been born into an old Boston Quaker family. Benjamin was a student of Walter Talbot, an instructor at the Philadelphia school of architecture, where Benjamin studied his craft. The religious beliefs and lifestyle of Talbot impressed Benjamin. He spent many hours at the Talbot family home, discussing slavery, war, women's rights and other issues. It was there that he met and fell in love with the strong-willed Rebecca Talbot, Walter's niece.

"Let's move into the dining room, where I'll continue with the Thompsons' history while we try out some Civil War-era furniture that once could have graced this home." They followed Jennifer into the dining room and everyone settled into high-backed chairs around an enormous black walnut dining room table.

"Not like having dinner on the couch in front of your favorite TV show, but not too stiff, I think," Jennifer commented as they arranged themselves. Various other comments were made on the comfort of the dining room chairs or lack of it, and Jennifer was asked a few questions regarding some of the room's accessories. Then everyone faced toward Jennifer for the story's continuation.

"Rebecca and Benjamin were married as soon as their house was ready for habitation in October 1839. They immediately began processing runaway slaves through their new home. In November 1843 their son Thomas was born. Still they continued harboring fugitives brave enough to risk fleeing slavery, though they never made their son privy to knowledge of those activities.

"In 1850, when Thomas was seven years old and his parents thirty-three, Rebecca convinced Benjamin to buy a sixteen-year-old slave named Annie from a neighboring farm. They immediately drew up papers freeing her and then offered her a position of employment within their household. Annie helped Rebecca run the house and care for young Thomas. While their initial relationship was somewhat that of a mother-daughter nature, it evolved into more of a sister or best friend bond. Rebecca and Benjamin spent evenings, after Thomas went to bed, teaching Annie to write, read and do math. But, in 1854, when Thomas was eleven and Annie—now Annie Free—was twenty, Rebecca died at age thirty-seven of tuberculosis. Her surviving family was plunged into grief but carried on without her. Benjamin continued Annie's education. Slaves still escaped from surrounding plantations and farms and needed harboring. Thompson continued to offer them harbor. He carried on as a solitary stationmaster until the Civil War began seven years later. He never shared his secret life with any of his family and they never discovered it, though his journals relate several very close calls.

"In 1856 the twenty-two-year-old Annie and thirty-nine-year-old Benjamin became lovers and on July 1, 1857, their daughter, Sarah Free Thompson, was born. Unable to wed legally, Benjamin Thompson treated Annie and their daughter with the same respect he had accorded Rebecca and Thomas. He never hid their relationship from his neighbors and the four continued to live as a family. That arrangement greatly angered some of Thompson's neighbors, particularly so as the Civil War drew near and then erupted in 1861, tearing apart families and communities. Some pro-slavery residents of the area had long suspected Thompson of aiding escaped slaves, though they could never prove it. One man in particular, Ruben Corey, who had remained an advocate of Maryland's secession from the Union, hated 'Thompson and his unnatural Yankee household,' according to an entry made by his wife, Catherine, in her personal diary.

"In 1863, fearing possible repercussions of violence aimed at Annie or Sarah, Benjamin decided, for their safety, to send them to Canada for the remainder of the War. On May 17, 1863, all was nearly ready for their scheduled May 18 departure. For her long trip northward, Benjamin wanted to surprise six-year-old Sarah with a little gray kitten, which she had been admiring for a few weeks. Feeling something ominous in the air that morning, he chose to leave her at home in spite of her pleas to go with him to the neighboring farm to pick up the kitten. To distract her, he showed her the secret room where he had hidden the dollhouse he had built for her upcoming seventh birthday. They made a pact that she was never to tell *anyone* about the room and was to play there especially quietly, regardless of anything else going on outside the room. It was to be a game in which Annie and Thomas made up the opposing team and whose calls she was not to answer. Leaving her with a bowl of apples and a pitcher of water, he promised to return before the morning was over.

"Since he didn't want to divulge the existence of the Underground Railroad room to either Annie or Thomas, he left for the neighboring farm letting them think she was accompanying him as she always did. I'm not sure how he managed that since there's no documentation on his movements after he left Sarah happily playing with her new dollhouse in her new secret playroom. But it seems he had probably originally planned on taking her as usual and changed his mind at some point during that morning and purposely neglected to inform his wife or son of the change. It's pretty clear from journal entries that Benjamin was most indulgent of his children and it would be consistent with his behavior to prefer not to leave Sarah crying and begging to go with him. So instead he set up an elaborate plan that allowed him to perform his errand, keep Sarah happy and protect Annie and Thomas from knowledge of the hidden room.

"Unfortunately, most of us can't predict the future and Benjamin couldn't foresee that his errand would separate him from Sarah and the rest of his family permanently. He successfully collected the kitten and was driving it home on their farm wagon, when he was overtaken by one or more people who shot him and left him dead or dying on his wagon, where it remained parked in the middle of the road between the two farms. The sheriff arrived at the Thompson home early in the afternoon leading the wagon carrying Benjamin's body and the mewing, caged kitten.

"Immediately a search was launched for the missing Sarah. And, of course, she was nowhere to be found. Josh Emerson reported that Sarah had not accompanied Benjamin when he came to the Emerson farm to pick up the kitten. There were no other farms between the Thompsons' and the Emersons', nowhere Benjamin could have safely left Sarah. She couldn't have been kidnapped before Benjamin got to the Emersons'. Two factors came into play that kept Annie and Thomas from finding Sarah for another two days. First, Sarah strictly followed her father's instructions of playing quietly, and second, the room had been carefully insulated to keep sound from penetrating through the walls.

"Try to imagine Thomas and Annie in their grief over the sudden violent loss of Benjamin, and having to face the additional probable loss of little Sarah—their tight family suddenly reduced by half. They must have been beside themselves with suffering, and yet they had to bury Benjamin—and do *what* with the plan of seeking the safety of Canada? They were left together in a kind of limbo in the house that had been their refuge. It became their prison. And as often happens in times of distress, they began taking their anger and pain out on each other. One evening, after Annie complained one time too many about Thomas' foul-smelling chamber pot, he stormed out of the house to find solace under the stars. Returning after a long walk in the moonlight, not ready to face the emotionally charged space between him and Annie, he stopped by the barn, sat upon an old stump and stared into the night. Why was she picking on him about the chamber pot? He had been faithfully emptying and cleaning it every day, just like she had taught him when he was seven. And it didn't stink! A faint light glowed from the roof and shone on the trees towering over the western side of the house. Something happened to Thomas as he sat there, grieving for the loss of his father and sister and for the resulting cleft between him and Annie. How could there be a light shining from the roof? The only thing up there was the failed skylight. Even if it worked, which it didn't, there was nothing lit in the living room that would shine up to the trees. *How could there be a light shining up from the roof? How? What could be the source?* Something unclear buzzed around in Thomas' mind. He jumped up and ran into the house, up to the second story and pounded on the door of the master bedroom. Annie came rushing out of the bedroom that had been hers before she and Benjamin became lovers. She had resorted to her old room because she couldn't stand the chamber pot smell permeating the master bedroom.

"Thomas hurriedly explained that the failed skylight was, in fact, reflecting light up into the trees and since there were no lights lit in the living room, it must be coming from the master bedroom directly above the living room. Together, they entered the large bedroom. There was indeed a strong odor of full chamber pot emanating from the closet. Annie and Thomas removed Benjamin's clothes hanging in there, and Thomas began pounding on the walls while Annie held a lantern to illuminate the tiny closet. With luck and persistence he fumbled upon the latch to the secret room where they found Sarah sitting quietly upon the floor, candle in hand, next to her dollhouse."

Smiling, Jennifer said, "I try to imagine that reunion. At least some of their suffering had to be alleviated by finding the child safe and sound. I try *not* to think about the possibilities of candle accidents and just be glad for them all that none occurred.

"In light of Benjamin's murder, Annie and Thomas thought it imperative to go forward with the prior plan of moving mother and child to Canada. Following their reunion in the secret room, the house must have been alive with their frantic activity in preparation for leaving. In their hurry to whisk Sarah off, her favorite doll was left behind. For reasons unknown, Thomas closed the door to the hidden room and never re-opened it." From the corners of her eyes, Jennifer glanced around at the people assembled at the table. With her mouth set into a grimace of distaste, not looking at anyone in particular, she added, "Well, his journal didn't say so, but he must have emptied the chamber pot because the one found in there when the room was rediscovered last fall was clean and empty. That must have been a lot of apples for a little girl to digest." Laughter and smiles erupted around the table then, as though everyone there had been caught up in the tension and grief tearing at Annie and Thomas and needed some comic relief to clear the air.

"They finished packing up early the next morning, and Thomas and a neighbor escorted them on the five-day journey to Canada. Annie and Sarah got settled there, and on December 3, 1863, Annie gave birth to Benjamin Thompson, Jr., great-great grandfather of the house's current owner. Annie, Sarah and Benjamin lived in Canada the rest of their lives. Thomas visited them at least annually and they corresponded regularly.

"In closing the door to the secret room, Thomas closed off more than just Sarah's doll. Benjamin had stashed money for the trip to Canada in a wall safe in the room; and all of his and Rebecca's personal journals, as well as carefully kept records, stories and anecdotes from their Underground Railroad days were found in *another* wall cache." She paused, giving everyone time to take that in.

"Thomas found he was unable to live in the house when he returned from Canada. Too much had changed. It brought up too much sadness for him. So he rented the house out for years. After his death, the Canadian part of the family continued renting it successfully through a trusted local management company until mid-1960, the very year that 'little' Sarah Free Thompson died—at the age of one hundred three. That year the tenants, who had lived here for three years, started complaining that the ghost of a little girl repeatedly visited them in the middle of the night. Their sleep was constantly interrupted and no one was able to either evict or console her. They left by the end of the summer; and without exception every tenant after them, frightened or frustrated by the ghost child who had seemed to have taken up permanent residence here, broke his or her rental agreement. For awhile—six months or so—no attempt was made to rent the house. But when a young couple, new to the area, asked for the house, the management firm drew up a lease. Again, the tenants were driven off. That sort of scenario repeated itself a number of times. At some point, the management company was acting more as a guardian of the house and grounds than as a rental agent.

"Last year the house passed to Sarah Louise Thompson, great-great-grandniece of Sarah Free Thompson. Before Sarah could get over here to inspect her inherited property, the ghost child began signaling the house across the street. She actually *solicited* help from the nearest neighbor, a girl new to the neighborhood. She spoke to her, told her the story of being left in the closet from the perspective of a six-year-old and asked for her help to find her lost doll. You can choose to believe that or not, but that girl's search for little Sarah's doll led to the discovery of the secret panels and the hidden room upstairs.

"When you continue the tour to the second floor, Sarah Thompson will be glad to give you details about the escaping former slaves who came through this house. She'll also be able to answer questions about how the history of the Thompson family was pieced together since she did a lot of the research for that history."

Before anyone could venture to ask a question or move to rise from the table, a loud commotion broke out at the top of the stairs. There was scuffling and someone spoke very loudly. "She took it! Didn't you see her? I thought they were part of the tour! Those people dressed in old clothes. Didn't you see them? Two white men and a black woman and little girl! They all had on Civil War-era clothes!"

Someone else said, "Oh them, they went out the back exit while you were talking. I thought you saw them leave. Weren't they part of the show?"

Downstairs a cloud passed over Tamara's face. "Sarah's doll?" she asked, shocked. "Are they talking about Sarah's doll?" No one answered her. "No!" she cried out in frustration. "No! That's Sarah's!" In a panic, she shoved her chair back and ran for the kitchen door.

At the street, she looked about wildly until she spotted the backs of the four people in fancy old clothing approaching the intersection. "No! Wait!" she yelled, running in their direction. At least they weren't running away. She could catch up with them and demand the ancient, fragile doll back. "Stop! Wait!" she called again as she narrowed the distance between them. Suddenly Tamara was tripping over a kitten, which had darted out of nowhere into her path. She couldn't maneuver out of the way and couldn't stop herself. She was going down and only at the last instant was she able to break her fall slightly with the heels of her hands. Ignoring the pain she looked toward her prey from where she lay on the sidewalk. At the corner the three adults all turned in

Tamara's direction and were *smiling* at her. *Smiling!* The younger man bent to pick up the child and when he stood, he was holding Little Sarah, beaming with delight, as she hugged Pearly to her chest. She looked straight into Tamara's eyes and smiled the smile Tamara had dreamed of bringing to Sarah's face. Their eye contact was brief yet timeless. Everything Tamara wanted Sarah to know was communicated within that fragment of time. Then the family turned and walked around the corner with Sarah holding Tamara's gaze until they were out of sight.

Felicia and Mary were jogging across lawns toward Tamara, calling out her name.

Tamara sat up and studied the tiny bundle of softness in varying shades of gray—from pale ash to charcoal to bluish silver—now mewing up at her from the comfort of her lap.

When her friends reached her, Tamara looked ecstatically up at them and told Mary, "You were right. She knew. Sarah knew." Then to both of them she said, "She has Pearly now. And she left me a thank-you gift." With her scraped and bruised hands, she picked up the tiny kitten. Holding it so that it faced her friends, she announced, "Meet Grace."

Printed in the United States
22271LVS00004B/703-705

9 781413 745764